HELLO FOREVER

hello
FOREVER

SARINA BOWEN

Tuxbury Publishing LLC

PRAISE FOR THE SERIES

A fantastic, unforgettable story! This book will make you cheer, cry, and swoon so hard! I adored it! - **Laura Kaye, New York Times bestselling author of the Hard Ink series**

"In a world of abundant romance novels, Sarina Bowen stands out." **Hypable**

"'Goodbye Paradise' is calibrated, controlled storytelling done with much panache and aplomb." - **Unstuck Pages**

"From the very first page I was hooked. I loved the story so much!!" - **Happily Ever After**

CHAPTER ONE

Axel

It all began on an ordinary Friday night.

The ordinary part was that I was home alone and settling in to watch a basketball game. And if my favorite team—the Chicago Bulls—had been playing that night, my life might not have changed.

The Bulls weren't on, though. And I was enough of a basketball nut to find another game to watch. I loved the sport in all its forms. College hoops? I'm there. A pickup game at the gym? Pass me the ball.

Basketball was my sport, my hobby, my obsession. But until that Friday night in November, I couldn't have said that a basketball game changed my life.

Now I could.

The game I'd chosen to watch wasn't even televised—I'd had to dig through several pages on the Barmuth University website to find a live-streaming link for the school's game against Northern Mass.

I'd wanted to see the Barmuth Brown Bears in action, because Barmuth U. in Henning, Massachusetts had just

1

into.

Might be getting into. I hadn't yet decided whether I was going to accept the position.

The job offer was in their athletic department, where I'd be employed on their budding sports-marketing team. In many ways it was my dream job. I loved sports, and I had a newly minted degree in marketing. Instead of trying to push toothpaste or insurance products, at Barmuth I'd be responsible for marketing the school's sports events to the community and to the college's wealthy alumni.

It sounded like a whole lot of fun.

On the other hand, Henning was a tiny, tiny town a thousand miles from my mother's home in Ohio. And it was two and a half hours from Boston and three and a half hours from New York.

For a young, gay, single man, the location was less than ideal.

Then again, I didn't have a lot of better options. I was living in my childhood bedroom, working an internship that did not pay. All of my friends had moved away from Columbus after graduation. There was really no reason to stay.

I was already lonely. How much worse could it be out in the woods in western Massachusetts?

My boyfriend had dumped me the day before we both graduated from OSU. "We're too young to be serious," he'd said. But what I heard was, *Later, sucker. Thanks for all the blow jobs that I didn't reciprocate.*

So there I sat, my face close to the computer screen, watching a basketball team that would probably never darken the door of the NCAA playoffs.

Barmuth was a small, private liberal arts university. It was

2

a lot of reading on the school's website, and it seemed like a nice enough place. They had an LGBTQ students' union, which was a good sign. And theoretically, liberal arts colleges in New England were as gay-friendly as any place on earth.

But would all that rainbow-powered goodwill extend into the dusty corners of the athletic department? That was my big concern.

At the end of my interview, my potential future boss had asked if I had any further questions. My last question should have been, "Will it ruffle any feathers if the new marketing person is as gay as a rainbow parade?" But I hadn't asked, because I wanted them to offer me the job.

The college's anti-discrimination policy would be wholly on my side, though there were no guarantees. And moving a thousand miles away to join a department full of strangers scared me more than I wished to admit.

On the screen, Barmuth scored a couple of three-pointers in a row. The team had some talent. I tried to imagine them as *my* team. In a month, I might be sitting at the officials' table, making notes for a boosters' press release and updating the team's Facebook page.

And here was a strike against Barmuth—the school's colors were an unfortunate combo of *brown* and white. I'd be sitting at that table wearing a brown tie.

But a guy couldn't have everything. At least the mascot was cute. I wondered who was inside that giant brown bear costume.

When the announcer mentioned the game's attendance was two thousand people, I cracked a smile. That was a far cry from an Ohio State game. But unlike my alma mater, Barmuth had offered to actually *pay* me for my labor. And working for

than ending up in a cubicle at some faceless corporation.

I leaned closer to my screen, as if the proximity of my nose to the video feed would make the decision easier. When the refs stopped the game to review a play on video, I got a closer look at the officials' table. There sat Arnie Diggs, the head of the athletic department. I recognized him from my Skype interview. He was an older man and the typical plainspoken jock.

Not that there's anything wrong with that. I just wished I knew whether he was a tolerant man. Would I feel welcome in his department?

He wants to hire you, though, I reminded myself. His judgment couldn't be *that* bad. Obviously.

The camera moved slowly across the stands, and I scanned the basketball-loving population of Henning, Massachusetts for clues. Could I make a life there? As the announcer yammered about a two-for-one special on pizza slices, I watched the crowd's faces.

It was right then that my night took a turn for the weird. Because one of those faces was *really* familiar.

He was in the third row. My eye snagged on a set of handsome cheekbones and a cleft chin. A face I'll never forget...

"Oh my God," I said aloud. *It couldn't be him*, my mind chided. But it really *looked* like him. Really. A lot.

Cax Williams.

Naturally, the shot cut away before I was ready. The camera went back to a view of the basket, and a player about to try for a free throw. But I was no longer interested in the players. They were just a blur to me now.

Instead, I sat there quietly freaking out, trying to decide if my subconscious had played a trick on me.

The last time I'd seen Cax Williams had been here in Ohio.

it I'd never told him so. We went to the same church retreats from third grade up until the awful day when I last saw him.

It had been Labor Day weekend, and the church diocese had rented out a girl scouts' camp to host the youth retreat. Cax and I had gotten caught doing something decidedly secular in nature. Although one of us might have said, "Oh, God."

We'd been on a church retreat, for fuck's sake. Not my sharpest hour getting caught with Cax in a liplock. The pastor in charge had stumbled across us in the woods. He'd had a proper fit and marched us into the office, where they'd yelled at us in separate rooms. Sin and hellfire and all that.

They'd also called our parents.

From what I could gather, our parents had vastly different reactions to our stupidity. After having stern words with my mom, the pastor had finally handed me the phone. And my mother had *laughed*.

"Oh, honey," she'd said with a giggle. "I'm so sorry to laugh. But you're going to have to work on being subtle. Do you want me to pick you up? The director said I could decide whether to bring you home a day early or to wait until tomorrow, like normal."

"I don't need to come home," I'd choked out. Not if I could stay one more night at camp with Cax. Even if they treated me like a convict, I still wanted to be near him. I needed to know if he was okay.

"All right, sweetie. Don't take their proselytizing too hard. And call me if you change your mind."

That was how I came out—or got outed. My mom, who'd raised me on her own and had hippie tendencies, had been typically cool about it.

But Cax? He'd disappeared.

5

dinner after another long lecture and a few threats. But Cax never returned. I'd spent the last twenty-four hours at the retreat watching for him, feeling devastated.

When I'd gone home, the news only got worse. I found that I'd been blocked from his Facebook account and from his phone. He never showed up at another diocese event.

Over the intervening years, I'd thought about him. I wondered where he'd gone, and if he was happy. I'd Googled his name a few times. But "Cax" was just a nickname. His real name was Henry Caxton Williams, and there were enough Henry Williamses on the Internet to populate a small country, so I never found a reliable hit.

Now, several years later, I could swear I'd just spotted him on camera in a tiny Massachusetts town.

For the rest of the basketball game, you would have needed a hammer and chisel to pry me away from the screen. Every time the camera panned the crowd, I squinted at the third row. I spotted my mystery man each time, but I'd need another close-up shot to decide if it was really him.

In the meantime, I tried to figure out who he was sitting with. On one side sat another guy, his head down, as if he were tapping on his phone. And on the other side sat a woman.

None of this told me anything. But all of it made me crazy.

Finally (finally!) there was another close-up of the team's bench. And there he was—his brown hair as thick and shiny as I'd remembered it. His gorgeous movie-star chin. That masculine, kissable jaw...

The broadcast cut to a commercial break, and another shred of my sanity flew out the window.

But wait! Now I could search for him on the Internet, because I had a little more to go on. I typed "Henry Williams Barmuth University" into the search box. A millisecond later I page at Barmuth.edu. *Henry C. Williams, Teaching Assistant, History Department.*

Hot damn. There he was, looking back at me from the department's website. I'd know him anywhere. The familiar, shy smile in the photo made me ache. It had been a long time since I'd allowed myself to wonder what happened to this boy who had accidentally broken my heart. I didn't realize I'd gasped until I heard my mother's voice.

"Axel? Is something wrong?"

I killed the browser tab so fast my thumb cracked on the button. "Nothing," I said, determined not to be caught stalking my first love. Didn't want my mom to know that six years later I was still thinking about the first boy I'd kissed. "Just watching a Barmuth game."

"Are they any good?" My mother stuck her head into the den and smiled at me.

"Um," I said, realizing I had no idea how the actual game was going. "They're okay. They'll be better when I'm working there."

Mom's eyes opened wide. "Did you decide? Are you taking it?"

"Yeah," I heard myself say.

She came all the way into the room and hugged my head in one arm. "I'm proud of you. But I'll miss you! Can I visit?"

"Of course." I hugged her back a little awkwardly.

"I worry about you."

"Why?" I chuckled. "Because I have no job, no friends and no boyfriend?"

Mom grabbed the back of my neck and shook me a little. "You *have* a job, but it doesn't happen to pay actual money. You *have* friends, who all moved to Chicago and New York. And your boyfriend was a dick."

"I hope you meet a *nice* boy in Massachusetts. That place might be a little lonely."

It might. But I'd already decided I was going, whether it was crazy or not.

CHAPTER TWO

Axel

One Month Later

My mother had warned me that every new job came with a few consecutive days of "what the fuck did I just do?" She wasn't wrong.

Even before I started the actual job, I ran into trouble. Just finding somewhere to live in Henning was tricky. The town was small, and I didn't want roommates. Also, November was half over. Housing in a college town is a lot like musical chairs —the music only stops every August and December. I'd missed the season when everyone moves in and out, so the few available apartments were the dregs of the lot.

And I didn't have a car. That was probably the last nail in the coffin of doom.

The first place I'd seen was a basement apartment underneath a professor's house. It smelled like damp socks.

Then I was shown a perfectly suitable place in a nice development, but it was so far out of town that I'd have to bike on a busy street with a narrow shoulder in every sort of weather. Taking my life into my hands during a snowstorm wasn't a

balcony overlooking an apple orchard.

Oh well.

By the time I made it to the last place on my list, I was pretty discouraged. The listing on Newbury Street was described as an "efficiency over the garage." That could mean anything, but I made an appointment by email with somebody named Caleb, and I showed up at one o'clock hoping for the best.

Newbury Street was pretty and lined with old houses. I liked it immediately. And when I knocked on number twenty-four, a really handsome guy came to the door to greet me. No —make that *two* really attractive men.

Hello, Newbury Street!

"I'm Axel," I said, shaking the first guy's hand.

"I'm Caleb, and this is Josh," he said, studying me.

"You're the owners?" I asked. They were both about my age. Too young to be homeowners.

Caleb crossed his arms. "Yeah. I'm a mechanic in the next town, and Josh is a student at the college. That's why we bought this place."

Well, damn. I guess I was just a slacker. "Good location," I said, trying to be friendly.

"Right," Caleb agreed. "The thing you need to know about your potential landlords is that we're married."

"To each other?" I said, sounding just a little more stunned than was polite. I didn't get a gay vibe off these guys at all. Then again, I'd known them for less than sixty seconds.

"You have a problem with that?" Caleb asked immediately.

"No." I laughed. "If I ever get married, it will be to a dude."

Caleb's face softened. "Oh. Any prospects?"

I shook my head. "Not a one. And here I am moving to a *really* small town."

"I'm not sure we should use the word 'apartment.' It's awfully small…" Josh warned.

Caleb clapped him on the shoulder. "Way to sell the place, babe. I don't think 'tiny living space' is going to impress anyone. Let's show Axel, and he can make up his own mind."

THEY NEEDN'T HAVE WORRIED. I liked it immediately. It was just a single long room plus a bathroom, but it had slanting ceilings, attractive wooden beams and a view of the woods. Staying here would be like living in a tree house.

"This table doesn't have to stay," Caleb said, pointing at the only piece of furniture. "But I left it here because it fits so well in this corner of the kitchen. I suppose you'd put your bed by the window, and there'd still be room for a couch to divide the sleeping space from the rest."

"A small couch," Josh corrected.

I turned slowly in a circle. "It works, though. And the TV goes there," I pointed at the wall near the door.

"Yeah," Josh agreed. "There's a cable hookup already, too. We just put it in."

"We bought the house a couple of months ago," Caleb explained. "It's a real fixer-upper. This apartment is in better shape than the rest of the house, if you can believe it."

"The house isn't *so* bad," Josh said a tad defensively.

Caleb turned to smile at his husband. "I'm not harshing on your house, baby. I'm just saying we have a lot of work to do."

"We weren't supposed to buy a house at all," Josh admitted. "We were living with friends in the country, and they would have put us up another year or two. We thought we were buying a second car so that I could commute to my classes at

excited."

"So now we have no second car, but we do have a mort-gage," Caleb finished. The words were somewhat ornery, but he put a loving hand to the back of Josh's neck.

I wondered if I was ever going to be half of a couple like that. They were so cute together that it almost hurt me to look at them.

Right. Stay on topic, Axel. "I, uh, don't have a car at all," I admitted. "The walk from here to campus wasn't too bad, but I was wondering if there's a shortcut...?"

Josh's eyes lit up. "That's why I wanted this place!" He moved to the window and pointed outside. "There's a path through the woods. This is actually the back of College Park. I never take the long way home anymore."

"You might during mud season," Caleb pointed out.

"True," Josh conceded. "But walking through the woods is a pretty awesome way to get to class. I'm loving it so far. Even when it snows, I'll just bundle up."

"Okay," I said. "Where do I sign?"

"Really?" Josh asked, sounding shocked. "That's awesome."

Caleb laughed. "Wait. Let's ask him all the important ques-tions. We can't deal with pets, unfortunately. And we have to do the whole background and credit-check thing."

"Go for it," I said. "One benefit of leading a boring life is that I'll pass your background check with flying colors." I pulled an envelope out of my back pocket. "And here's my offer of employment from the college." I passed it to Caleb.

He opened it up and scanned the letter. "The athletic department, huh? Well, your salary seems pretty straight-forward."

"Yeah, except I'll be the least *straight*forward person in the athletic department."

that?

"Does it show?" I asked, and he laughed.

He handed my letter back. "Come into the house and you can fill out the application."

"My mom is willing to co-sign the lease," I offered, following the two of them out the door.

"That probably won't be necessary," Caleb said.

I took one more glance at the sunny little room before I closed the door. At least one thing in my uncertain life looked to be shaping up. Even if they hated me at work, I'd have a nice place to go home to.

CHAPTER THREE

Axel

Walking in for my first day at work was nerve-wracking—my first real job out of college.

My credit card was maxed out from purchasing a bed and a sofa before I returned the rental van. If I couldn't fit in here, it was going to sting. And I'd be poorer than before I'd tried.

The athletic department occupied a modest suite of offices adjacent to the gym. The athletic-ops people and the marketing department shared a bull-pen style room, while my boss Arnie's private office was a few yards away down a short hallway.

My desk was one of two along a wall. The other desk belonged to a ham-necked man-child who introduced himself as "Boz," which was short for Jon Bosworth.

Boz had decorated our office space by tacking Barmuth Brown Bear sports paraphernalia onto every available surface. He was the other half of the sports-marketing department, so we were going to be partners.

He was, I decided, the most rabid Barmuth sports fan who had ever lived. As far as I could tell, Henning, Massachusetts was his favorite place on earth. He'd graduated from Barmuth

ment the week after tossing his mortarboard in the air.

In fact, the centerpiece of all the wall-mounted sports glory above our desks was his football team photo. Beneath his beaming face was the captain's "C" stitched onto his team jacket.

"Welcome!" he'd said about a hundred times on my first day. He sort of galloped around the room, making sure I had a stapler and a tape dispenser on my desk. It was possible that it had been Boz inside the Barmuth Bear suit I'd seen in the basketball TV broadcast. He was a frisky human. He was the sort of jock who referred to a beer as a "brewski" and not in an ironic way.

Every hour that passed made me more worried about how he was going to react to my sexual orientation. I'd already decided not to hide. I wanted this job, but I wasn't willing to duck into the closet to keep it.

Casually slipping my sexual orientation into a conversation with Boz the Barmuth Brewski Bear was not going to be easy. I was tempted just to shock him. *Hey, would you happen to know where the nearest gay bar is? I could really use a rim job.*

Luckily, I was saved from making semi-rude statements that might get my ass kicked by spending most of the day at a new-employee orientation and filling out a giant stack of forms for the human resources department.

On my second day of employment, Boz and I had our first actual conversation about sports marketing.

"So," he began with a lazy grin. "You've doubled the size of my department. Dude, that's awesome."

"Um, yeah." I gave him an awkward smile.

"Obviously, I've had to triage all the work up to this point," he said, rubbing his scruffy chin. "The football team takes up a

teams. But I'm just one guy."

"Gotcha." And I really did. On any given weekend, there were three or four sporting events at least. Nobody could cover all of that.

"So, we need to divvy up the teams. I mean, I'm calling football, on the grounds that I have seniority..." He frowned.

"Of course," I said quickly. "Football is all yours."

"And you're the basketball guy, right? So I should probably take hockey, because of the season overlap."

"That's cool." I liked hockey, but he was right about the schedule. "And it goes without saying that we should each cover the men's and women's teams for each of our sports. Otherwise, it's just too confusing."

"Sure." His grin morphed into something naughty. "We might have to flip a coin for volleyball."

"Why?" I thought volleyball was awfully lame. He could keep it.

His eyebrows shot up. "Dude. Tall girls jumping around in short shorts?"

Shit. This was my opening—the moment I was supposed to tell him. If I let this opportunity pass, I'd be stepping into the closet, which was ridiculous. I'd been out since high school, for God's sake. "Uh, Boz?"

"Yeah?"

"Women's volleyball isn't really my thing. Actually, *women* aren't really my thing."

His monobrow furrowed. "Seriously?"

"Seriously." I braced myself for a clarifying slur or a fit of disgust.

"You mean..."

You're a faggot, is what I thought he would say next.

17

cheerleading?

A surprised bark of laughter escaped my chest. "It's all yours, man. And field hockey. And gymnastics if you want it. But you should let me take soccer. I don't have a fall sport yet."

"Deal." He grinned like a kid on Christmas. "Let's make a list." He reached for a pad of paper, but then checked his watch. "Dude, it's gettin' towards quittin' time. What if we made this list over at Bruisers? If I don't eat regularly, I get cranky."

"Okay?"

"I mean, if I'm going to work overtime, there needs to be a burger or a beer involved. One or the other, preferably both." He stood up and yanked the Barmuth Football jacket off the back of his chair. I stood up to follow him.

And that was the whole story of my coming out at work. Or rather—I thought it was. The messy part wouldn't come until much later.

I SPENT the rest of that first week learning how our mailing list and social media accounts were organized. As Friday approached, I started to get excited for my first men's basketball game. I was really looking forward to it.

Boz had given me a little talk about our hours. "You'll be working late on Friday. The game won't end until 9:30, prolly."

"Right?" That didn't bother me at all. Because basketball.

"So you gotta take the afternoon off. I mean, this job has irregular hours. If you work your forty hours *plus* hit three sporting events a week? *Boom!* All of a sudden you're working a fifty-five hour week. Don't set that precedent, man. It's not

Unlike Boz, I had no life in Henning. A fifty-five hour week wasn't much of a hardship, but I didn't want to be the new guy who showed up the older guy. So I took his suggestion and left work a little early on Friday, hitting the gym for a quick workout. And when game time came around, I was itching to get down to business.

Henning was a small school, and the basketball arena only seated three thousand people. But I still felt like I'd won the lottery by getting this job. Taking a courtside seat at the officials' table felt as glamorous to me as walking the red carpet on an awards show.

I was getting *paid* to tweet about basketball. Pinch me.

Since my set-up was crucial to my success, I checked and re-checked my Internet connection, and I made sure that the graphics and the video snippets I'd assembled were in the folder where I'd left them. This had to go well. I wanted the guys in the athletic department to say, *"I'm so glad we hired that marketing guy. He is such a stud."*

Okay, that last bit was a stretch. But I wanted to do well.

And there was nothing like a live sporting event to get my blood pumping. The seats began to fill behind me and across the gym. We were playing Princeton, which was a major Barmuth rival.

Directly beside me, the announcer picked up his mic. "All rise for the national anthem, sung for you tonight by Barmuth's very own Barmuth Baritones."

As I rose, a group of twelve guys wearing tuxedo jackets formed a half-circle on center court. One of them raised his hands, and they all began to sing the Star-Spangled Banner in four-part harmony.

straight.

I filed that away to think about later. Because after the anthem and a few announcements, the game began. I put a hundred percent of my attention on the players in front of me. A minute after the tip-off, a Barmuth player scored on a break-away, and I made my first ever post to the @BarmuthBBall account. *It's game time here in Barker Arena, and #14 Josh Bramer puts Barmuth on the board!* I followed that up with a tweet linking to the radio station covering the game and another link to the live-stats website.

Just like that, I was on the board, too.

Hunkering down, I watched the action as if my life depended on it. I was so invested in getting things just right that I actually forgot to look around for Cax. I didn't think about him at all for the first ten minutes of play. The game paused for a media time-out, and I sat back in my seat, actually sweating. That's when I heard it.

His *laugh*. Goosebumps broke out on my arms. Rich and hearty, it was amazing how well I knew his laugh. As if I'd heard it just yesterday. He might have been laughing at a fart joke I made when I was twelve, or some silly thing I whispered during the church service. The sound of him was so achingly familiar that I had to close my eyes just to take it in.

And he was sitting somewhere behind me.

Welp. There went my concentration. Luckily, tweeting a basketball game isn't exactly neurosurgery. I'd prepared so ridiculously well ahead of time that I had plenty of material. Princeton led for a while, but when we retook the lead, I tweeted a little video clip of a tiger running into a wall.

The most difficult thing, though, was keeping my face forward. I wanted to turn around so very badly. I was like Orpheus in that Greek myth where he has a chance to lead his

turn to see her face.

Orpheus fucked that up and lost the girl. But I stayed strong. I knew that if I started staring at my teen crush, I wouldn't be able to stop.

The game seemed to last about a hundred years. Near the end, I hadn't heard Cax laugh for a long time, and I actually convinced myself that he'd left. So I held out until there were only two minutes left on the game clock. Barmuth had a seven-point lead, and Princeton took a time-out, which followed on the heels of a media time-out.

My job here was nearly done. So I finally turned to look.

CHAPTER FOUR

Caxton

"Why can't I have Skittles? They're only two bucks," my youngest brother said for the seventeenth time.

"Because you had a soda. That's enough sugar," I told him yet again.

"I wouldn't have had the soda if I thought I could have Skittles," Scotty argued. He was twelve years old and a junk-food hound.

"Next time," Amy said, mussing Scotty's hair.

He wrinkled up his freckled nose and turned away. But he didn't complain about the hair mussing, because Scotty liked Amy.

Everybody liked Amy—my brothers, my asshole father. Amy was a real crowd-pleaser. "Are we going out for a beer after I drop the boys at home?" I asked her. I'd had a long week, and I was looking forward to gossiping with her.

I heard a snort from my other side, where my seventeen-year-old brother Jared sat. "'Out for a beer?' Is that what we're calling it these days?" He said this without raising his surly face from his phone.

Amy and I exchanged an amused glance. It was hard to

said was a sexual reference? Or that Amy and I would take any opportunity to have sex?

The reality was that we hadn't had sex in years, and we'd only done it twice before she'd very gently pointed out that we didn't seem the least bit compatible.

I sure as hell wasn't ever going to correct my brother's assumptions, though. The fact that everyone thought Amy was my girlfriend made my life a lot easier.

But we were just very good friends. With us, "out for a beer" really meant out for a beer. But when basketball was in season, we could often be found here on game nights, in the company of whichever of my brothers wanted to get out of the house. Tonight we had Scotty and Jared—two out of three—because Mark was at a middle-school dance.

Jared had barely said a dozen words all night. Seventeen was a surly age, to be sure, but I wondered if something was bothering him. I'd have to remember to ask him later in private.

Amy nudged me.

"What?"

"That guy..."

I looked to see where her attention was focused. But the man I thought she was looking at turned his head sharply back toward the game. "What about him?"

"Well, I've never seen him sitting there before."

"Uh-huh." I'd never paid much attention to the guys at the officials' table. Not when there was a game to watch.

"And he was staring at you."

I said nothing. Because I didn't know anybody who worked the games, and I didn't want to say even one word that put "guy" and "staring" in the same sentence.

Our team scored a three-pointer, and the crowd went nuts.

felt more comfortable.

"Did you see that?" I asked Jared, nudging him with my elbow.

He gave me a teenaged caveman grunt, which was all you could get out of Jared sometimes.

On my other side, Amy grabbed my wrist. We'd been friends a long time, and it was obviously a signal. My eyes flicked immediately to the man she'd pointed out earlier.

And my heart absolutely stopped.

For a long moment I locked eyes with none other than Axel Armitage, the only boy I'd ever kissed. But he wasn't a boy anymore. Not by a long shot. I was staring at a man—a very attractive man with dark, wavy hair and big eyes. He'd filled out over the years. His shoulders were square and muscular, and a five o'clock shadow highlighted the contours of his masculine jaw.

I forgot the basketball game. I forgot Amy and my brothers. There was only the memory of his smile in the summer sunshine and an ache in my chest for what had happened the one time I'd acted on my longing.

The sound of a whistle shook me out of my stupor. Axel's head whipped back toward the game, and I tried to swallow the giant lump in my throat.

Amy nudged me. "You know him?"

"Later," I said. There was no part of the story I could tell Amy in front of my brothers.

WHEN THE FINAL BUZZER SOUNDED, I stood up like a shot. "Let's go, guys. It's a school night." I grabbed Scotty's coat and held it out for him.

25

"Um, I knew that," I snapped. "But it's late. Let's go."

Amy gave me the side eye, but she didn't argue. In fact, she helped me herd my brothers out to the car.

"Are we having that drink?" she asked as I cranked the engine.

"Oh hell yes."

Jared snickered in the backseat.

Whatever. I drove my brothers to the home they still shared with my asshole of a father. "Night, guys," I said as I pulled into the driveway. "Give Mark my love. And if you need anything before I see you on Monday—"

"—call," my littlest brother finished. "We know."

"Love you both," I said as they climbed out.

"Love you, too," Scotty said. "Thanks for the game."

"Anytime."

"Yeah, thanks," Jared muttered. He did not say "I love you, too," of course, because he was too cool for that. But I didn't mind. I said it to him because I needed him to know that I cared, and because my father didn't do emotion. (Unless anger counted.)

Amy rolled down her window to say goodnight, too.

It had been a mistake to pull into the driveway. Before Jared and Scotty made it inside, the kitchen door opened and my father stepped outside, a garbage bag in his hand. He thrust it at Jared. "Forgetting something? I told you hours ago to—"

"Sorry," Jared said quickly. He grabbed the bag and high-tailed it toward the garage.

His hustle made me incredibly uneasy. Jared was a stubborn teenage boy and not exactly the model of obedience. He wouldn't be so eager to please unless the cost of pissing off Dad were really high. It made me wonder—not for the first

always been verbally abusive—that went without saying. But the whole reason I'd moved back to this town after graduation was to make sure he wasn't also physically harming them.

I sure hoped he wasn't. And that if he did, my brothers would tell me.

"Something the matter?" my father asked, and I realized he was staring at me through Amy's open window.

"Not a thing," I said quickly. And then I felt like kicking myself. My own eagerness to get out from under his attentions was still showing, even though I hadn't lived in his house in years.

My father turned and went inside without wishing me good night, and Amy rolled up the window.

I found myself letting out a giant sigh.

"You okay?" Amy asked.

"Sure," I lied. The truth was that my head was spinning. One look at Axel had me tied in knots.

"Who was that guy at the game?"

I put the car in reverse and backed out. "Are we headed to Bruisers?"

"We could," she hedged. "But why don't you come over instead? I'll open a bottle of wine."

"Done." At the end of the cul-de-sac I turned left instead of right, and two minutes later we pulled up in front of her family's mansion.

Amy and I had both graduated from high school in Henning. We'd dated during our senior year. In fact, it was in this very house that she and I had awkwardly lost our virginity to one another.

The sex had been utterly underwhelming for both of us—nobody saw fireworks. We'd tried once more in the back of my car, and that had been even worse.

the fodder for a million inside jokes between Amy and me. Second, it proved to me that sex with women was not my thing.

After graduation we'd gone on to different colleges, but we stayed tight. That's how strong our friendship was. We'd failed miserably at giving each other orgasms, but we were really good at watching basketball together.

And? She'd never told a soul what she knew about my sexual orientation.

Now Amy led me by the hand through the foyer of her stately home. "Hi Dad!" she called as we passed the library.

"Hi, pumpkin."

"Hello, Professor," I said, feeling the latent guilt that any guy feels walking past a man whose daughter he's deflowered.

"Evening, Cax." His newspaper didn't even twitch. The mood at Amy's house was always this calm. No wonder we'd always hung out here and never at mine. I loved this place.

It was a little weird to see Amy pouring wine at the kitchen counter, something that had never happened when we were teenagers. She and I had both moved back to Henning after graduation six months ago. She had a job in the admissions office, and I was a graduate student. She lived at home to save money. I lived in graduate student housing because I couldn't share a roof with my father. But I'd chosen to go to school here because I realized my brothers still needed me.

Push and pull. That's how this town felt to me.

I carried the wine into the cozy TV room at the back of the house. She clicked the TV on to a crime drama but left the sound low. By silent mutual agreement, we sat close together on the sofa. "Okay, spill," she said immediately.

Ack. I took a deep drink of wine to stall. "His name is

in Ohio. And then when we were sixteen, we fooled around."

Her eyebrows shot up. "*Really?* You never told me that."

I never told anyone that. "It...didn't end well. We got caught. The pastor called our parents."

"Oh." Amy's stricken face was proof that I didn't need to fill in the details. She'd met my asshat of a father.

"Yeah. I never went back to any more of those church retreats, obviously. And my father stood over me while I blocked Axel on Facebook and my phone. We left Ohio less than a year later."

Amy sipped her wine, looking thoughtful. "So you haven't seen this guy's face in how many years?"

"Six and a half," I said quickly. *But who's counting?*

"And now he's here in Henning."

My heart thudded just to hear the words. "And working at the basketball game. Unless he was here with the other team."

Amy grinned. "He was wearing a brown tie, Cax, and sitting on our team's side of the table. There's no chance he's with the other team. Wait—I think you both play for the same team!" She cackled at her own joke.

Meanwhile, my stomach took a long tour through my midsection. The idea that Axel Armitage might live in the same town made me feel lightheaded. I could bump into him in the coffee shop. Or the *gym*... Visions of Axel dribbling a basketball in very little clothing flooded my brain.

Jesus Christ. This was not good.

"I think you should call him," Amy announced.

"No way."

"Way! Because otherwise this will all be incredibly awkward. I mean...the last time you saw him, you were both naked?"

"Not *naked*," I said quickly.

29

good time naked with *someone* in your life. At least once."

Sadly, I shook my head.

"That's just plain wrong. You're twenty-two years old. You should live your *life*."

It's not that I didn't want to. But it just wasn't an option. My father would beat the shit out of me if he found out I was...with a guy. So if I ever wanted to date, it would have to be somewhere far away from here. If not for Scotty, Mark and Jared, I'd be out of this town faster than you can say, "So long, suckers."

But I had three brothers who needed me. And Scotty was only eleven. That meant at least six or seven more years of solitude.

God, how depressing.

"It's not so bad," I lied. "And who's to say that I'd find somebody, anyway? It's a small town. I mean...you're sitting here with me tonight, right?"

"Well..." Amy cleared her throat. "There's something I need to tell you."

My stomach bottomed out. *Again*. Because I knew what blow she was about to strike.

"I met someone."

"Wow, that's great," I heard myself say. "Who is it?"

Her pretty face took on a shy smile. "He works for the I.T. department. I've been having, um, a *lot* of computer problems at work."

I laughed for the first time in an hour. "You are adorable. And I've heard those I.T. nerds are awesome in the bedroom."

"Cax!" She gave my knee a shove. "Don't mock."

I caught her hand in mine. "Amy, I'm happy for you. Really." It was true, too. Even though I knew I was in trouble, because this would change things. Amy couldn't be my "date"

30

people think we were a couple.

"We'll still have basketball games," she said, reading my mind.

"Only if you want to," I said quickly.

"Of *course* I want to. We have season tickets together. Jeez."

"Your new guy might not like that you have season tickets with your ex."

She swirled the last of the wine in her glass. "Well, I was thinking about that. No guy is going to love the idea of his new girlfriend hanging out with her ex. But if he understood that we were *really* not compatible..."

I shook my head immediately, and she sighed.

"Okay. It was just a thought. Because there's really no reason why we shouldn't hang out as much as we want." To prove it, she turned to stretch her legs out over mine.

I grabbed the insteps of her stocking feet and squeezed. Amy loved to have her feet rubbed. We knew each other so well. It killed me to think I was losing her company to some I.T. guy. But I wanted her to be happy.

"I'm worried about you," she said.

I only grunted my response.

"Are you going to call Mr. Church Camp?"

"No way," I said quickly.

Her eyes widened. "Why not? I thought you used to be friends?"

"I can't." It really was as simple as that. If I wanted to be with my brothers, I had to stay in Henning. And if I wanted to stay in Henning, I had to hide that part of myself from everyone. (Everyone except Amy.)

"You could just be friends again," she said softly.

sure that he's..." The sentence died on my tongue.

"*Gay.*" Amy crossed her arms. "Why have I never heard you say that word?"

I shrugged, but it was a fair question. Though Amy couldn't possibly understand how holding a core piece of yourself back from the world required incredible concentration. The word felt like a spell to me. If I said it, all my hard work would slip through my fingers.

"So are you going to call him?"

"No."

"Omigod, Cax. You're hopeless."

I was saved from agreeing with her by her father. "Amy!" he called. "Derek is on the phone!"

I hadn't even heard it ring, but it was hard to miss the look of joy on Amy's face. "Derek, huh? That name isn't as nerdy as I feared." I pushed her feet off my lap. "Go talk to your guy. I'll let myself out."

Amy leapt up. "I love you, Cax."

"I know." Using my foot, I gave her a little shove on her ass. "Just go, okay?"

She hustled out of the room to take her call. I washed both of our wine glasses in the kitchen. And then I went home to the graduate dormitory alone. Like I always did.

CHAPTER FIVE

Axel

As the final buzzer sounded, my boss Arnie sat down beside me. "Hey, kid. How's it goin'?" I hadn't even known he was in the gym.

"Great," I said, practically bouncing in my chair from tension. I knew I'd done well at my first game of the season. "Let me show you what I've done." I swiveled the screen of my computer in his direction. "Our new basketball Twitter stream has game commentary, links to the video stream and athletic department articles."

"What's this?" he asked, pointing at a GIF.

"Uh, a little video snippet of a tiger crashing into a wall. I posted it when Princeton was down by ten."

Arnie threw his head back and laughed. "That's a little ridiculous. But I like it."

"So did my audience," I said. "That was my hit of the night. It was shared a hundred times."

His eyes widened. "*Really?* A zoo video?"

"Really."

Arnie chuckled. Then he stood up and clapped me on the

up with when we play the Terriers."

It wasn't a bad moment with my new boss, but while I'd been chatting him up, Cax Williams had apparently left the arena. I turned around and he was gone, along with the people who'd been seated beside him.

Finished for the night, I closed my laptop with shaking hands and shoved it into its case. There was too much adrenaline in my body. Seeing Cax had practically knocked me over. Then we'd stared at each other like a couple of imbeciles.

I put on my coat and backpack and walked out into the night. Tonight I didn't mind my lack of wheels. I needed the walk home to calm down. The park was deserted, of course. I'd wondered if the path through the woods would feel creepy at night, but it didn't, really.

When I'd told my mother about my commute through the woods, she'd promptly FedExed me a headlamp from LL Bean. I'd tucked the funny little device into a pocket of my backpack just in case. But I'll tell you right now that a man cannot look sexy wearing a head lamp. Not even Channing Tatum could pull that off.

Either way, I didn't need the lamp tonight. With the moonlight reflected off a dusting of snow on the ground, there was enough light for me to see my way, and soon I was home, unlocking the door to my quiet, barely furnished apartment.

I got ready for bed in silence, bringing my tablet with me when I slipped beneath the sheets. I considered watching a movie or listening to some music, but I set the tablet aside instead.

What I really wanted to do was think about Cax.

I'd met him at a wintertime church retreat when we'd both been eight. We'd made friends in that desperately fast way that

looked at each other and smiled.

After twenty-four hours, it was obvious to both of us that we'd done well to end up together. A couple of the other boys were crybabies and a couple more were bullies. Cax and I were the nicest of the lot, in our own opinions, anyway.

We both had Xs in our names. It was meant to be.

Every two months or so our diocese offered a youth retreat, where kids from three or four churches in our half of the state would meet up for activities (some fun, some lame) and prayer. My single mom liked to send me on these, because it meant she could go out with her friends for a night. One of us prayed while the other drank half-price beers at a roadside bar.

Until I met Cax, I only tolerated these trips. But after we became friends, I enjoyed them.

Often the retreat took place from Saturday overnight until Sunday. They had us in sleeping bags on the floor of some church's all-purpose room. But in the summertime there was always a four day "camp" to attend. Those were my favorite.

Over the years Cax and I did everything together—archery, swimming, horseback riding. Sledding, marshmallow roasting. Bowling. Wherever we were, I always brought my basketball in the hopes that there would be an available hoop.

Cax had never played hoops before we met, but I taught him all my grade-school moves. Whenever the church leaders planned something really boring—like gluing macaroni on paper plates in the shape of a cross—I'd give him the eye and we'd sneak outside for a little one on one.

Rinse and repeat. By the time we hit our teen years, we were the kind of friends who texted. On social media, I saw occasional pictures of Cax's life at a fancy private school in the suburbs.

close, though our paths never crossed except for at the regional youth gatherings.

Because of basketball, I didn't make it to as many of the church events during my teen years. But I always made time for the summer camp retreat.

The summer I was sixteen, I had begun to admit to myself that I was gay.

When June rolled around, I was happy to see Cax, as usual. But that was the year my interest in him changed. When Cax climbed out of his family's late model Range Rover on drop-off day, my heart practically exploded. Because...*damn*. He'd shot up and filled out a little. And when he turned to smile at me, his dimples did something to my stomach.

For the first time since I'd met him, I didn't know where to put my eyes.

I'm sure I said something witty like, "Hey, man." But a sixteen-year-old boy isn't expected to be eloquent. And whatever he'd replied, I hadn't heard, because my poor little brain was struggling under the weight of an uncomfortable realization.

I was very attracted to him.

We set up the tent that Cax had brought for us to share, and I tried to snap out of it. Somehow I got through dinner and the bonfire on that first night of camp. But I could feel his presence like a heat inside my body, my awareness of him hot enough to roast marshmallows.

It wasn't the first time I'd ever wanted to stare at a guy. I'd already figured out that my appreciation for the athletic photography in *Sports Illustrated* was different from my friends' in a few crucial ways.

And the swimsuit issue? Not interesting to me.

But until then, I hadn't felt so *confronted* by the truth, and

wanted to touch and pale eyes that made me stare at him. That first night, I'd barely slept. The second night I had to jerk off quietly after I was positive he'd fallen asleep.

Swimming together became a new form of torture. Watching him strip off his shirt made me dive for cover in the lake. I had to keep my towel nearby on the dock and beg and plead with my body to stay under control whenever we changed into our suits.

My teenage hormones were raging, and at night it took me forever to fall asleep. Because he was right there—two feet away. I'd never been so aware of another person's body in my life. Each breath he took echoed through me. Each rustle of fabric reminded me of our proximity.

The third night I woke up in the pitch dark, and I wasn't sure why. Sleeping on an air mattress in a tent meant lots of unfamiliar noises. For a few moments, I lay there silently, listening.

But it wasn't footsteps or owl hoots that had woken me. It was Cax. His breathing was a little funny. Short and shallow. I listened, and there was a rustle, too. A repetitive one.

My heart rate leapt when I realized what I was hearing. Cax was jerking off.

The nice thing to do would have been to lie there in silence and pretend to sleep through it. But I couldn't do that. Just the idea that he was getting himself off made me painfully hard. My hand slipped into my boxers against my will. I squeezed my aching dick and let out a sigh.

Beside me, Cax froze, so I did, too. But I was too horny to give up. So tentatively, I stroked my cock again, thinking of him. Wishing the hand on my dick was his. The pitch darkness gave me the illusion of freedom. As long as we didn't speak or see each other properly, I could pretend it wasn't weird. So I

slowly, hoping he'd continue to do the same.

After a minute, he did.

Cax is a leftie, and I'm not, so our elbows bumped once. Twice. The darkness and my arousal made me bold. I moved my upper arm so that it brushed against his, skin to skin.

He leaned into my touch, and I held my breath for several beats of my heart.

Now, years later, it was hard to imagine that I'd been brave enough to take it further. But lust is one hell of a powerful drug.

Slowly, I'd rolled onto my side, facing him. I'd shoved my boxers down all the way, then grabbed his working wrist with my free hand. I waited to see if he'd yank it out of my grasp. But he didn't. So I slid my palm down until my hand covered his. Then I gave it a squeeze. In my mind, I was almost touching his dick.

He gasped, and again I waited for the panicked withdrawal. Instead, he began to stroke himself in earnest, with my hand there as back-up. When he rolled to face me, I got even braver. I knocked his hand away and took his hard dick in my hand.

"Fuck," he whispered in the dark.

The word gave me heart palpitations. But I didn't let go. He was so hot and sturdy in my grip. I loved touching him. It was the highlight of my horny teenage years. I took a chance and swiped my thumb over his cockhead, and he hissed.

Damn, the sound of him just made me crazy. I wanted more. I wanted as much as I could possibly have.

With a low moan, I inched closer, my left hand jacking him. I felt one of his hands land on my chest, heavy and warm. I grabbed it and moved it immediately onto my aching cock.

Cax sucked in his breath when he first touched me. I was terrified he was going to stop this. Stop *me*.

hand down my length and lovingly fingered my balls. My heart seized up with surprise. Then he used both hands to jack me off—one cupping my balls, and one to slide up every aching inch of my dick and over the too-sensitive head.

The only sounds in the tent were our fast, shaky breaths. I wanted to touch him everywhere at once. I was on *fire*. I gave my hips a snap, fucking his fist, and he let out a quiet little moan.

"Fuck," he whispered again. But his voice was full of awe, not fear.

Rocking my hips like crazy, I chased my bliss. And thirty seconds later I came like a fountain. One second after that, he did, too.

Then there was only panting and guilt as we wordlessly and in vain tried to wipe spooge off ourselves and our sleeping bags.

We didn't say a word to each other, which should have been weird. But oddly enough, I slept quite well after that.

The next morning, we didn't speak about it, or even make eye contact. I wanted to reassure him, but I was afraid. We went to breakfast and sat beside each other without comment. There was hiking. There was swimming. We did all of this without discussion.

But after lunch we were assigned "reflective time." Following the buddy system, we were sent into the woods, two by two, to sit quietly and reflect on the subject of heavenly love.

Nobody thought it weird that Cax and I were buddies. We'd been partnering up on this stuff for years.

That day would be the very last time we were together, but as we walked into the woods, I hadn't any clue. We followed first one path and then another, until everyone had fanned out

39

in sight. And then Cax led the way over to a rounded, flattened rock, where he sat down.

Without asking for permission, I sat beside him. I couldn't go home tomorrow with this silence between us. I knew I needed to man up and say something.

But he beat me to it. "Well," he whispered.

"Well," I echoed.

"That was...nuts."

My response was to snort loudly and embarrassingly. Because *nuts*.

He got the joke, too. Then we were just two sixteen-year-old idiots laughing into our hands.

Eventually I got control of myself. "I'm sorry," I whispered. "I didn't mean to freak you out."

His eyes shifted nervously. When he spoke again, it was almost too soft for me to hear. "But I liked it."

Hearing that should have made me giddy, but his face was so fearful. So, being a good friend, I tried to let him off the hook. "So did I. But blowing a load is always likable."

He gave his chin a short-tempered shake. "No, I *really* liked it."

My heart palpitations started up again. "Like, enough to do it again?"

He kept his eyes on his shoes. "Yeah."

Nobody had ever made me as happy as he did right then. That's the only explanation for how stupid I was immediately afterward.

First, I let out a shaky, disbelieving breath. Then I reached over and palmed his chest, right over his heart.

He looked up at me with fearful eyes, and I didn't know what to do. Here I had all this joy, and he was afraid of how he felt.

bone. "Don't be sad."

He gave a long, slow blink. Once again, we were too close to each other for me to ignore my feelings. I leaned forward just a couple of degrees.

Cax matched it.

And then I kissed him. It was the first time I'd really kissed anyone. So the shock of his lips against mine was almost too much. I'm sure I moaned. He leaned in, his lips parting beneath mine. I slipped my tongue inside.

Heaven. He tasted of everything I ever wanted. His tongue slid warm and wet across mine, and I wrapped my arms around him to get as close as I could.

We kissed and then kissed some more. And because we were horny teens, our hands began to wander until we were rubbing each other through our shorts.

It was just too amazing. Too much. Too consuming to hear the approaching footsteps on the path.

But I *did* hear the angry gasp of the pastor who'd found us. And the rough sound of his voice when he demanded that we stop that instant and follow him back to the camp office.

Cax didn't look at me at all on the walk back. That's how I realized how badly I'd fucked up.

"This is a church camp," the deacon said over and over when they'd put us in separate rooms to dress us down. "You have sinned against God and made a mockery of our mission."

"I'm sorry, sir," I said. But what I really meant was, *Please don't be awful to Cax.*

It wasn't until years later that I'd realized I'd had no need to cower—that I might have argued when the pastor called me a sinner. How dare he shame me over some kisses? Even worse —I hadn't had to let Cax go without saying how I felt. I could

to me.

But I hadn't done any of those things.

Instead, I'd let the man lead me back to the office, where he separated me from the best person in my life and called our parents.

It wasn't until much later that I remembered the last thing I'd said to Cax. *Don't be sad.*

But after that day, I definitely was.

CHAPTER SIX

Axel

Since spotting Caxton at the basketball game, I'd become more conscious of the fact that I might run into him just anywhere. I began to look for him when I crossed the quad or when I was standing in line at the coffee shop.

It took a while until we bumped into each other, though.

One of the nice things about working for Barmuth College was the fancy-ass gym. Renovated a couple of years ago, the place was practically a temple to fitness. There were row upon row of cardio machines and a well-stocked weight room. Other offerings included an Olympic-size swimming pool and courts for basketball, squash and tennis.

Since I had no social life, it made the most sense for me to go to the gym after work. Fridays were my favorite—the undergraduates were off eating dinner or making their weekend plans. The gym was gloriously empty.

The Friday after I'd seen Cax at the game, I decided to run two fast miles on the treadmill to warm up. I needed the workout. I needed the flex and tug on my muscles and to blow off some steam with my pounding feet. Work was going fine, for

easy. And I was lonely as all hell.

After some stretching, I found a vacant leg press and loaded it up with plates. Sliding onto the seat, I tightened my abs and pushed. The foot-piece moved with the ease of a well-maintained machine, which was how I felt, too. Exercise was like therapy. A good workout always cleared my head.

I was three sets in when, in my peripheral vision, an attractive set of back muscles clenched as some fabulous creature pressed a bar over his head. I wasn't there to stare at guys, but what I saw pulled me in. Sandy-brown hair. Broad shoulders. Gorgeous biceps tensed against the sleeves of his T-shirt. *Yum.* There was something very familiar about his stance, so I turned my chin for a better look.

My heart lurched when I realized who I was looking at. *Cax.*

I turned away again to try to get a grip on myself. I wanted to talk to him so badly. But after the basketball game, he'd disappeared immediately—a bad sign. Then again, I'd probably given him a shock.

I'd spent the last week wondering what kind of a life he was living now. He'd been at the game with a woman. His wife, maybe? Kids had been seated with him, too—but they were too old to be *his* kids.

I'd been turning this over and over in my mind. Maybe our time together had only been experimentation for him. Perhaps he was a straight, married man who didn't want any kind of reminder that he'd once hooked up with a dude, even if we'd been kids ourselves at the time.

But even if that's how things were, I still wanted to say hello. I'd never embarrass him with tales of our teenage years. Maybe I needed a chance to say that.

caught him watching me.

Here goes nothing.

I slid off the leg press, gave it a quick wipe with my towel, and headed across the weightlifting area to where he stood near the squat rack. His eyes widened as I approached. He looked fearful.

Shit.

"Hi," I said in a friendly tone.

He hesitated for a beat. "Hi."

We stared at each other for a second. "Look," I said. "I know it's weird. But this is a really small town. I just moved here."

His gaze dropped to the floor.

Jeez. I talked fast so I wouldn't chicken out. "I don't have any idea what you're thinking. But we have two choices. We can pretend we were never childhood friends. Or we can go out for a beer and catch up. It doesn't have to be a big deal."

When he raised his eyes to mine again, there was so much panic there that my heart gave a squeeze. "I'm sorry," he said softly.

"For what?" Was he trying to tell me that we couldn't even have a beer together? Really?

"For, uh…" He looked over both shoulders, as if he were checking for eavesdroppers. And I had to hold in my sigh. "I guess we do need to catch up on a few things."

"Okay. How about Bruisers? It's the only bar I've been to yet." Boz had taken me there the other night, and I'd found it to be a laid-back sports bar.

He licked his lips nervously, drawing my attention to his mouth. "I don't… I'm not sure Bruisers is a good idea."

Ouch. My old friend was either paranoid or embarrassed to be seen with me. He couldn't be seen having a drink with a

next suggestion flew out before I had time to think about it. I'm pretty sure I made it just to challenge him. "Okay. My place then? Tomorrow night? Seven?"

He swallowed hard. "Where is that?"

Honestly, I hadn't expected him to take me up on the offer, and it was possible he didn't plan to follow through. He might blow me off. "I live at the end of Newbury Street just as it dead-ends into the park. The house is an old white one with a wrap-around porch. You can't miss it. But I live in the apartment over the garage."

"Okay," he agreed.

"If you need my number, I'm in the employee directory. Athletic department."

He nodded. "I'll find you."

I really hoped he would. And wasn't that pathetic? "Actually, come hungry tomorrow—I'll make dinner. You bring a bottle of whatever you like to drink."

"Good plan. I will."

I didn't know whether Cax drank or not. There were so many things I didn't know about him. I wondered if that would change. "See you tomorrow at seven."

I walked away before he could reconsider.

CHAPTER SEVEN

Caxton

I had never been so nervous about anything. Ever.

Apparently, a case of nerves turned me into a vain person. I showered and shaved more carefully than ever. And then? I spent half an hour trying on shirts and staring into the inadequate mirror on the back of my tiny closet's door. It was a total waste of time, since I ended up wearing the one I'd put on first.

Ridiculous.

Axel and I had shared a short and horribly stilted conversation at the gym last night. I'd sounded like the world's biggest asshole. And it was all because of nerves.

Nobody had meant more to my young life than Axel. Nobody. I'm sure I never told him that.

Growing up in my father's house hadn't been fun. Mr. Military Man didn't tolerate weakness of any kind. His favorite put-downs were *faggot* and *pussy*. In his eyes, any small failure meant you were one or the other. Or maybe both.

Nothing I ever did was good enough for him. He pushed me to go out for football, but I couldn't hack it. Never liked it. But it was years before he'd let me quit. And since my father

school, my dad's influence and disapproval seemed to pour into every corner of my life.

Church retreats had been different.

The church was my mother's domain, and it had made her happy to see me involved there. And since my father could hardly argue against holiness, my interest in the youth group had been above reproach.

Axel had been my truest friend, and the only person in my life who I ever allowed to see my weaknesses. Since he wasn't part of my painful life at school, he didn't know I was bullied. He didn't care if I couldn't throw a spiral.

The reason I played basketball with him was because he made it fun. It didn't matter that I wasn't very good at it—not at the beginning, anyway. Axel didn't give a damn whether I was a worthy opponent. He always wore a smile while he was holding that ball.

His enthusiasm had been contagious. And I swear that my new-found ability to play hoops had saved me from more of my father's wrath. The sport was *almost* manly enough for him. He'd let me switch to basketball when I was thirteen. And since I wasn't completely hopeless at it—thanks to Axel—he'd decided it was good enough.

Axel had walked into my life holding a basketball when I was eight. And without even knowing it, he'd made my life at home more bearable.

I'd known I was gay at a very early age, well before I knew what the word "gay" meant. I think I'd been around ten when I'd first realized I wanted to kiss Axel. Or the actor Elijah Wood. One or the other.

By the time we were teens, Axel had become everything to me. My friend. My savior. My crush. I'd kept that last bit to myself, but not because Axel would be horrified. Somehow I

ings—or acting on them—had never been an option.

When we'd been sixteen, for one shocking and glorious day I'd had everything I'd ever wanted. That day in the woods Axel had said, "Don't be sad." I'd wanted Axel more than I'd wanted my next breath, but, even then, I'd known it wouldn't last.

I'd been proven right about five minutes later. And after that awful moment of discovery, I'd done what I'd needed to survive. My father had kept one of his army boots firmly planted in my back all the way through high school. He would rant against "homos" and "faggots," and I knew his speeches were directed at me.

So was his violence.

My friendship with Axel had been collateral damage. I'd turned my back on him to save myself, and I owed him an explanation. No wonder I was nervous about this dinner. The tension was killing me.

I left for his place a few minutes early just because I couldn't stand it anymore.

The walk to Axel's house made me feel even nuttier. I didn't drive, because I was too paranoid about someone spotting my car in his driveway. A driveway at the end of a dead-end street. That was crazy even for me. I was an adult who was free to have dinner with anybody on the planet. And Axel and I were going to be *friends*, nothing else. But I felt so transparent when it came to him. Like anyone could look right through me and see how I felt about him.

How I'd *once* felt about him. A lot of time had passed.

Walking the edge of College Park to get to his street, I realized there was probably a shortcut through the woods. But I'd been practically speed-walking, and I needed to slow my pace or I'd arrive at his place unfashionably early.

The street brought me to an interesting old house with

started up the driveway. My progress was halted by someone on the house's front porch. "Hey, Professor Williams!"

Joshua Royce stood in the glow of the porch light. He was a student in the History of Agricultural Economics course where I was a teaching assistant.

Somehow I found my voice. "Joshua. Evening." My neck got hot. "This is your house? I was just..." *having a panic attack*.

"Yep, we bought this place a few months ago." He leaned over a stack of firewood and collected an armload of wood. "Visiting Axel?"

"Yeah," I admitted, trying to make it sound like no big thing.

"Cool." He gave me a funny smile. "Glad he's making friends already. Have a nice night!" He turned and went back into the house.

I stood there for a minute in the dark, wondering what the hell had just happened. This was *exactly* why I needed to stay the hell away from Axel. My feet itched to turn around and retreat. But before I could take a step, a door swung open in the building next to the house. Light spilled over the stairs leading to what looked like the garage's second floor. "Cax?"

The sound of Axel's voice was all it took to unstick me. Without my permission, my body moved toward the person I wanted to see most in the world.

I took those stairs in a daze, following Axel into the apartment at the top. The first thing that hit me was the smell of something wonderful cooking.

"My place isn't much," he said, reaching for my coat. I handed it over. Then he headed over to a tiny excuse for a kitchen as I shut the door behind me. "But I liked the location."

"It's...nice," I said. And it was. The room wasn't large, but

something in the oven, and I found myself admiring the way his ass filled out a pair of dark-wash jeans.

Stop, I chided myself. Staring at men's butts was something I did all the time. It was the only sex I ever got, and therefore I felt entitled. But I couldn't stare at *that* ass—on the only man I'd ever touched. Just thinking about what we'd done in that tent all those years ago made my pulse jump and my cock grow heavy.

Moving on. I took a deep breath and thought of my father's angry face. That always did the trick.

Beyond the kitchen and dining table, there was a small, two-seat sofa facing a rather nice wall-mounted TV. And on the far wall, a generous row of windows looked out on the moonlit pines. He'd put his bed over there. That's what I would have done, too.

I looked away, because there was no way I could think about beds while I was here. There were precious few places I could comfortably rest my eyes while standing in a room with Axel.

There was snow dripping off my boots, so I kicked them off and carried the bottles I'd brought over to the counter. "I brought you a couple of local beers." I lifted a four-pack onto the counter. "And a bottle of red. That's my drug of choice."

Axel turned around and smiled at me, which was a real shock to my system. *Damn*, that smile. "Can I pour you a glass?"

What was the question? "Um, thanks."

He opened a drawer and pulled out a corkscrew while I tried not to notice the muscles flexing in his arms. "Actually, can you open 'er up? I need to make a salad dressing."

"So..." I cleared my throat. "You cook, huh?"

"Sure. You?"

roommate in college who did all the cooking. I tell him all the time that it's his fault I'm helpless."

Axel laughed. "Sounds pretty handy, actually. Anyone special?"

It took me a minute to understand the question. "Oh—*no*. Not like that." I felt my face reddening at the idea. My roommate Gil had no idea about me. Even after four years of living together.

Axel began whisking a bowl of oil and vinegar. I watched him, feeling as though I was having an out of body experience. He was both incredibly familiar and terribly strange. Axel had bulked up, and I sure did appreciate the view. But I could still see the skinnier teenager that he'd once been.

Trippy.

I cleared my throat. "Are you going to tell me what brings you to Barmuth? I mean...obviously basketball. You always loved basketball."

He turned and shot me another smile, this one so gorgeous that I knew I'd be taking a cold shower later. "Yeah, I never got over my obsession with hoops." He chuckled. "I work for the athletic department in marketing. I'll be covering soccer and lacrosse, too."

"Wow. That's a cool job. But why Barmuth?"

Axel looked down at the counter and bit his lip, which seemed like an odd reaction. "Well, they offered me a job. And nobody else did. Every guy wants to talk about sports for a living, I guess. There aren't a lot of openings."

My answer was a reflex. "Not *every* guy."

He laughed. "Fair enough. Anyway—I'd never spent any time in Massachusetts, and I didn't really know what to expect. But there was nothing keeping me in Ohio. After graduation, my boyfriend dumped me and my friends all moved out here."

My boyfriend. Well, that answered that question. Axel liked men. I felt another tightening in my groin just picturing Axel with a man. Axel unbuttoning another man's shirt. Axel's hands on a man's chest.

Jesus. Time to talk about sports again. "Your degree is in marketing?"

"That's right. So what do *you* do here in town?" he asked.

That was safe territory. "I'm a graduate student in Economic History. So I'm taking courses for a year before I start doing research for my dissertation. And I'm working as a teaching assistant. In fact, your landlord is in my section of an econ class."

Axel looked up in surprise. "No shit? Josh is your student?"

"Truth." I must have looked nervous then, because Axel left his whisk alone and gave me an appraising look. "You didn't want to run into anyone you knew tonight, did you?"

God, am I that transparent? Slowly, I shook my head.

Axel gave his dressing one more stir and then poured it in a thin stream over the salad. "Did you know that Josh is married to a man?"

"What?"

Axel grinned down at the salad bowl. "His husband is a mechanic named Caleb."

"I didn't..." I stammered. "I couldn't tell."

My ex-best-friend stopped tossing the salad, leaned his hip on the counter and crossed his arms. "Hey, Cax?"

Hearing him say my name turned my stomach into jelly. "Yeah?"

"I don't really have you figured out yet. But you look fucking terrified over there. I didn't mean to freak you out by asking you over. I was just trying to be friendly."

though."

His face fell. "Will you tell me about it?"

"I think I have to."

He opened the oven and pulled out a pan. "Okay. Let me serve this up, and you can tell me all about it while we eat."

I peered over the edge of the pan. "God, that's beautiful. What is it?"

"Chicken breast stuffed with feta cheese and lemon zest."

"Wow." My mouth watered even before he'd finished the description.

"And twice-baked potatoes." He grabbed a pair of tongs and lifted a piece of chicken onto a clean plate. Then he added two halves of a twice-baked potato and handed the plate to me.

I stared down at the beauty on the plate. "Damn. I don't even know what to say."

"Say you're hungry. Let's eat."

WE SAT down at his little table, where Axel lit a candle. (A candle! What man does that?) But damn if he didn't look even more attractive with that soft glow on his face.

I lifted my wine glass and tried to relax. I was basically living out my fantasy right now—a private dinner with a ridiculously attractive man. A glass of wine. A secret hour without interference from the depressing forces in my life.

"What have I missed?" Axel asked, slicing into his chicken. His gorgeous eyes flicked up to mine. "Tell me."

Reality caught up to me pretty fast when he asked that question. But I took a bite of his excellent cooking to stall. The chicken was tender, with gooey, salty cheese and an herbal

swallowing.

He grinned. "Every food is made more awesome with melted cheese. It's just a fact."

"True." I took a fortifying sip of wine. "Okay, my father made my life hell after our incident at camp." I knew I was blushing now, but there was no way around it. "That's when he started slapping me around. He cut me off from a lot of people after that. Not just you."

Axel had stopped eating his dinner. "I'm so sorry, Cax. Seriously..."

I held up a hand to silence him. "It's not your fault. Nobody should ever take responsibility for my father's actions. If I've learned anything in the last few years, it's that."

"Okay," he whispered.

"He's still barely civil to me. After I got home that summer, I spent months just trying to stay out of his way. Then, about ten months after I last saw you, my mother died of liver cancer."

Axel's eyes grew large. "I'm *so* sorry."

"It was a long time ago. But it made my life complicated, because I have three younger brothers."

"I remember."

"Everything at home changed really fast. My mother died a few months after her diagnosis. My father didn't get any nicer. He transferred here to Barmuth."

Axel leaned forward in his chair. "Here? You finished high school in Massachusetts?"

"Sure did. And all my brothers still go to school here in town. After high school I went away to B.U. for four years, because I wanted to get away from him."

"Right. Why would you stay?"

Mark and Jared."

"Your brothers."

"Yeah. That's why I decided to do my PhD at Barmuth. My brothers need someone around who isn't an asshole. They don't have a mom. Scotty was only six when she died." This was some really depressing shit I was unloading on him. "As far as I can tell, my father doesn't hit them. I think he saved that just for me. But his mind games are pretty bad..." It was hard to talk about this stuff. The only person who ever heard these things from me was Amy. "Anyway. By the time I'm done with my doctorate, Scotty will just be turning eighteen."

"When is that?"

"About six years from now."

Axel nodded. "You live at home?"

"Oh *hell* no," I said, and Axel laughed. "Actually there's exactly one perk for being my father's son—my graduate housing is half price because he's an employee of the college."

"That's handy."

"This whole setup only works because I don't have to live under his roof. But I pick up Scotty from school most days. And I ferry the kids to some of their after-school crap."

He grinned. "And to basketball games."

"Yeah. I have five season tickets."

"Who's the fifth one for?"

I felt my face get hot. "Amy."

He cocked a single, sexy eyebrow. "Your girlfriend?"

Slowly I shook my head. "She's my ex," I said. And that was technically true. But I was hiding a lot behind that statement.

"You two must be close."

"Yeah," I practically grunted. I'd been pretty depressed since Amy told me about her new man. I knew it wasn't rational, but I felt like I was losing my friend.

were beautiful in the candlelight as he studied me. I could tell he was fishing for clues about my sexual orientation. And damn if I wasn't flattered. Again—it was my dream come true. Dinner with a gorgeous guy who might be trying to figure out if I was available.

But dreams were for other people.

"No," I said slowly. "I don't date. I can't." I took another bite of his excellent cooking. This was the only dinner he'd ever cook for me. I might as well enjoy it.

"Why not?"

I had to dig deep to find the guts to answer. "Well...this doesn't leave the room, okay?"

His face dropped. "You can trust me."

"Um..." I gave a nervous chuckle. "Amy will be the only girlfriend I ever have." It was difficult to meet his eyes, but I managed it. And in his expression I felt warmth reflected back to me. "But if I want to have contact with my brothers, I can't...date anyone else," I said. "The old man lets me do a lot of his childrearing. But if I lived my life the way I want, he'd cut off contact. And I wouldn't be able to keep in touch and make sure they're being treated well."

He set down his drink. "That is damned depressing, Cax."

"I know. But it's only six or seven more *years*." I knew I sounded bitter.

"*Jesus.*"

There was a sad silence at the table. Having unburdened myself, I ate the last of my chicken.

"I'm sorry you're in such a bind," he said softly.

"Thanks. It is what it is. People have lived through worse."

"So when I need to know if there are any gay bars in the Berkshires, I shouldn't ask you?"

My heart stumbled over the idea of Axel out on the prowl,

gay bar. Sorry."

"I don't think I'm going to find one here, anyway," he said quietly. "But maybe you could tell me instead—where should I go in this town? I mean generally. And, well, where *shouldn't* I go?"

That was a good question. "Not like I'm an expert on the subject, but the town of Henning is a pretty safe place to be queer. Ten miles in any direction it's pretty rural. But still— this is Massachusetts. The most liberal place on earth."

He grinned. "Good to know. What else do you like about the place? Tell me what I need to know."

"Fine—the bookstore has the best coffee. And the people-watching can be good there." I lifted my eyes to his and smiled. It was hard to believe all the private shit I'd told him tonight. But after the disastrous way our friendship ended, it felt good to tell him why. And now I had a new confidant. Trusting him was easier than I thought it would be.

"Thanks." Axel chuckled. "That's exactly the kind of tip I'm looking for."

"The diner out on Route 11 is excellent, but I don't make it over there very often."

"I don't have a car," he admitted. "I don't want to spend the money until I'm sure the job is going to go well for me."

"Why wouldn't it?"

He pushed his plate away. "You never know. It doesn't *feel* like the athletic department is staffed by homophobic assholes. But it's a small department at a small school in a small town. I can't just assume that I'll fit in anywhere."

"Oh." This was just the sort of complication that staying in the closet helped me avoid. It was really the only perk of denying myself the life I wanted.

"The people I've met so far seem okay, though..."

forgotten how easy it used to be with us. How we could shoot the shit for hours. Our conversation wandered to marketing and then TV shows...

I could have sat there all night. But eventually Axel pushed back his chair and carried his plate to the sink. "Stop right there," I said. "I've got the dishes."

"You don't have to do that," he protested.

"But I want to." I carried my plate over, too. Then I put a hand on his shoulder and gave him a playful nudge out of the way.

He turned to me with a smile that I felt *everywhere*. "Fine. I'll pour you another drop of wine. You're not driving, right? I didn't see a car."

"Right." *Because I'm paranoid about my car being spotted outside your home.* I was such a shit.

I washed the dishes and Axel dried. I drank my wine standing there in his kitchen, trying not to let my eyes drift over his body. I knew I couldn't sit on the sofa with him. I didn't trust myself.

When the glass was empty, I set it on the counter. "I really should go. But this is the most fun I've had in a long time." Why not tell the truth, right? It's not like I could make a habit of this. Too risky.

Axel must have sensed my martyrdom, because he looked a little sad. "Glad you could make it."

"Me too." I grabbed my coat off the doorknob and put it on. I stepped into my boots. But then I stood there, unsure what to say next. *Thanks, but we can't do this again?* Was this really it between us? Forever? That seemed impossible.

While I tried to make sense of it all, Axel stepped closer. He was watching me carefully, probably trying to figure out

59

door.

The closer he got, the more aware of him I became. The masculine breadth of his shoulders seemed to loom in my consciousness. I wanted to reach up and measure them against the length of my hands. The dark shadow of his evening whiskers begged me to reach out and touch his chin. How rough would it feel under my fingertips?

I knew I should turn and open the door. But I just couldn't make myself do it.

His face softened as he took a half step closer. The distance between us was mere inches now. "Goodnight, Cax," he said softly.

Me? I said nothing. I'd been rendered speechless and motionless by all of my desires.

Axel let his right hand drift over to take mine. I might have managed to turn it into an awkward handshake. And I think he was trying to let me do that.

But I closed my fingers around his hand and squeezed.

In response, Axel gave a tug, pulling me toward him, letting go only when we were chest to chest. I felt his hands slip under my jacket and land on my waist. Every cell of my body waited for him to kiss me. I wanted it so badly.

I froze as Axel tipped his head, sighing as his lips moved in to graze my jaw. Goosebumps rose on my chest as he placed a single soft kiss at the corner of my mouth. "Mmm," he breathed. Then he kissed my cheekbone. Then the side of my nose. His breath ghosted over my skin, and I screwed my eyes shut, waiting.

And then I couldn't take it anymore. I turned a fractional degree and found his lips with mine. And...*goddamn*. His lips were both soft and firm as we found each other. The kiss was so...*tender*. I'd spent a half hour telling Axel my life story

again in an instant. As our lips slid together, everything I'd ever felt for him hummed between us.

His mouth softened, and I took advantage, slipping my tongue between his lips. I was so greedy. He tasted of red wine and *man*.

Six years I'd waited for this to happen again. I moaned, and my hands found his chest as I leaned against him. That firm, wonderful chest.

"What do you want?" he whispered between soft kisses.

But of course I couldn't answer. I never gave words to my desires. That gave them too much power. I moved my hands around to his back and pulled him closer. My cock was already heavy and hard.

"What do you want?" he repeated. He took one of my hands and placed it over his cock, which felt as hard as mine. God, I wanted him so, so much. I gave him a firm stroke and he groaned. "I'll tell you what I want," he said, kissing my chin. "I want to drag you over to that bed and find out if you're a top or a bottom."

That's what woke me up.

"I can't," I gasped, jerking my body backward. "I can't be either of those things." My chest was heaving, and my whole body was hot. But I couldn't keep pretending that this was okay. Finally, I did what was necessary. I spun around, opened the door and went outside. "I'm sorry," I muttered. "I have to go."

Horrified at my erratic behavior, I couldn't even make myself turn to wave goodnight. The cold air was bracing, and I welcomed the shock of it on my overheated body. Above me, the door closed, but I couldn't think about that right now. I couldn't let my mind go back to those moments with Axel. To my ridiculous behavior.

I took it.

Wandering around in the woods at night should have been a stupid idea, but there was a good moon tonight, and it lit up the snow between the trees. The path was a dark stripe heading toward campus. So I hurried toward my crappy little room in the graduate dorm.

It was what I had to do.

CHAPTER EIGHT

Axel

A week later, I woke up feeling lonely as fuck. It was Saturday so there was no job to go to. That should have been a blessing. But I had no friends, except for the one I'd kissed after he specifically told me that he couldn't get involved.

That had been stupid of me. *So* stupid. I could have had one friend in Henning, Massachusetts, but now I had none.

I put on a few layers of clothing, my iPod and my running shoes, and pounded out two miles around the neighborhood. When I was done showering, it was still only nine thirty.

There wasn't even a basketball game on to watch.

So I did the next best thing—I baked a batch of muffins. I'd used my favorite recipe, which was pear and ginger. I ate three of them, gobbling them down with a cup of coffee.

I was going to gain twenty-five pounds if I kept this up.

Leaving myself three more muffins for tomorrow, I put the other half-dozen into a plastic tub and carried them down the stairs to Caleb and Josh's back door. When I knocked, the first thing I heard was a hair-raising shriek. Confused, I couldn't decide whether to knock again or walk away. The door jerked open to reveal Josh standing there with two very small children

muffins?"

"I didn't know you had babies." I stepped inside.

"What babies?" he asked with a wink. "Oh, you mean *these?*" He hitched them both up a little higher as I shut the door.

"NOT a baby," protested one of the little people in his arms.

"That's right," Josh agreed, kneeling down to set her on her feet. "You're a big girl. So stop taking toys away from your baby brother."

She ran out of the room without a backward glance, and then a third small person toddled into the room, grabbing Josh around the knee.

"Hello, miss," Josh said. "Say hi to our new neighbor, Axel."

The little girl squinted up at me. Then she buried her face in Josh's leg.

He laughed. "This is Willy. She's my cousin Miriam's daughter, and the other two are my cousin Maggie's kids. We spend a lot of time together. Miriam and Maggie are out shopping together right now."

"Wow," I said. "Do you do this every Saturday?"

"Pretty much. It gives their mothers a break."

"Have a muffin," I said, putting them down on the counter. "I realized I was going to chow the whole dozen unless I gave some away. They're pear and ginger."

Josh's eyes widened. "You baked? In that little kitchen?"

"I've cooked in worse kitchens than that one."

"Wow. Neither Caleb or I are true cooks. I mean...we get by. But it's a lot of burgers on the grill and macaroni and cheese from a box." Josh reached down with his free hand, broke off a piece of a muffin, and shoved it in his mouth. Then his eyes rolled back in his head. "Oh jeez. Yum." He broke off

The baby moved his little face to the side, refusing it. "More for me," Josh said, popping it into his mouth.

I eyed the whole crazy scene with a smile on my face. There were toys on the floor, and the sound of cartoons coming from the living room television. But Josh looked unruffled. He pointed at the coffee pot on the counter. "Want a cup? You'll have to pour for yourself." His hands were busy with the baby-holding and the muffin-eating.

"Sure. Thanks." I really didn't need more caffeine, but I wanted to linger a little longer, and Josh wasn't hurrying me out the door. I took a mug from the cupboard he indicated and poured my cup. There was a carton of milk on the counter and I helped myself to a splash.

He plunked himself down in a kitchen chair. "It's crazy here today. You'll probably think twice about knocking again."

"No way. My apartment has that new-guy silence."

Josh nodded slowly. "You made one friend, though, right?"

My stomach tightened. "You mean..."

"Professor Williams." His lips quirked into a little smile.

Shit. "It's not like that," I said with a sigh.

"No?" He looked surprised. "I just assumed that when a guy shows up at dinnertime with a bottle of wine under his arm..."

"It's not like that," I repeated. If Cax needed to play the straight man in this town, I wasn't going to wreck it for him.

"Too bad," Josh said. "I would have put money on him being gay. He is, right?"

Inwardly I cringed for poor Cax, who would not want to hear that one of his students had assumed he was gay. "Well." I swallowed. "He's better off if we don't try to speculate. There are people in his life who might not be okay with it."

"Oh." Josh's face fell. "I know exactly how that works. Say no more."

"I didn't see a thing," Josh said, eating the rest of the muffin one-handed while the baby drooled on his shoulder. "How do you know him, anyway?"

Now there's a story. "Back in Ohio we used to be friends, but he moved away in high school." I left a few crucial plot points out of that summary, of course.

"No way! So you do know someone in town."

Yeah, and I kissed him, and now he's not speaking to me.

"Hi guys!" a male voice called from the living room.

"In here!" Josh hollered.

Caleb appeared in the doorway. "Hey! What's up?"

"Axel baked muffins. Get in here and try one of these." Josh lifted the container for Caleb.

"No shit?" He reached for one.

"Language," Josh scolded. "What is Chloe doing in the living room? It's too quiet."

"Watching Elmo. And taking apart the cable modem with a screwdriver."

Josh rolled his eyes. "You crack yourself up."

"Every day." Caleb leaned over to kiss Josh on the head, and that small gesture made my heart ache. Would I ever have someone of my own?

Caleb sat down and told us about his shift at the garage. He and his coworker had made bets on whether a third coworker had proposed to his girlfriend the previous night. But when they called him to verify, they'd learned he'd walked in on her with another man yesterday after work.

"Oh, *man,*" Josh said. "That is rough." He picked up a baby's bottle off the table, tucked the baby boy into the crook of his arm and offered the little guy the nipple.

The way Josh cared for these kids so effortlessly was mind-boggling. I wouldn't know what to do with a baby if it sat up

feeling myself staring.

"Isn't it weird?" Caleb said cheerfully. "More coffee?"

I stood and washed my mug. "I should get a move on," I said. "Leave you guys to your Saturday."

"Come for dinner some night next week," Caleb offered. "It's not usually this crazy around here."

I smiled at him over my shoulder. "I don't mind the crazy. But we will do dinner. That sounds like fun." I put my mug on the drying rack.

"Thanks for the muffins!" Josh called.

"You can stop over with these anytime," Caleb teased.

"Later, guys." Smiling to myself, I went up to my quiet little treehouse residence. For want of something better to do, I logged in to check my work email. There was one message, from a personal email account called "Caxtrastrophe."

DEAR AXEL,

I could only find a work email for you. But I needed to say thank you for dinner. It was terrific, and I haven't had that much fun in a long time.

I also wanted to say I was sorry for flipping out and running off without explaining myself. That was pretty ridiculous. You probably think I'm nuts. When I said I didn't get out much, I obviously wasn't kidding.

Hope you have a great weekend,
C.

I SWITCHED to my private email and wrote out a reply.

· · ·

Don't apologize. You told me the rules. I heard you loud and clear, but then I went looking for loopholes.

Sorry to put you in such a tough position. I won't do it again. Unless you want me to. *Slaps self.* Okay, that wasn't helpful. I'll try to be good.

Axeldental

I HIT "SEND" and hoped that our friendship could be resuscitated. Yet my conscience nagged at me. I'd never stop wanting him. And I'd never stop trying to figure out how to have him.

There had to be a way.

CHAPTER NINE

Caxton

Winter arrived, bringing another foot of snow to Massachusetts. I wrote two papers for the classes I was taking and graded papers for the class where I was a T.A. Joshua Royce wrote a good paper about the history of dairy farming in New England. I gave him an A-.

He never mentioned my visit to his tenant's apartment, and I sure never brought it up.

Sitting in a library carrel after office hours, I made some notes about a manuscript I was reading, while making periodic checks of my private email account.

These days, I checked the damn thing every five minutes like a love-sick teenager. I knew I was being pathetic. It's just that I couldn't help myself.

For the past few weeks, Caxtastrophe and Axeldental had exchanged dozens of short messages. Except for those first two, where we apologized to each other, there wasn't a lot of weighty content. Instead, everything we said to each other was light and funny. Friendly.

And *flirty*. But not in a dirty way. Axel didn't send pictures of his dick or anything. Instead, he'd send pictures of his

in marinara sauce and mozzarella. *Hungry? There's plenty*, he'd written.

Of course I'd begged off, my excuse being the Bulls game that had been on TV. I'd sent him a picture of my feet propped up on the coffee table with the TV in the background.

I'd wondered if he'd ask me when I'd become a Bulls fan. When we lived in Ohio, the Bulls were his team, while I hadn't been much into basketball at all. I only played at church retreats because Axel liked it so much. It wasn't until after we moved away that I began to follow basketball in earnest.

Because it made me think of him.

But when he'd replied, Axel hadn't mention the Bulls. *Oooh! How did you know I had a foot fetish? Just kidding. Nobody really has those, right? I mean, nobody who's ever sniffed my basketball shoes.*

We traded emails all the time now. Just like that, his chatter became part of my life again, and it made me ridiculously happy. Ours was an odd, electronic friendship. We were twenty-two-year-old pen pals who lived only two miles apart. Pretty pathetic, but I didn't dwell on it. Because being his pen-pal was my only option.

Can I ask a question? Axel wrote one evening. *What does your dad do for work here in town? And how does he manage to keep his foot on your back now that you don't live at home? Sorry if that's too personal a question. You don't have to tell me.*

I'd preferred our light and flirty emails. But I answered it nonetheless.

HE WORKS FOR THE COLLEGE. *He runs their ROTC program and teaches a course on military history.*

And as for the other question, I'm aware that he can't really keep

out with the boys. And he just laid it out—a threat. If my "faggot ass" was with a man, I'd never see my brothers again.

Do you have any idea how hard it was for me to write that? Because I <u>know</u> it's ridiculous. He shouldn't be able to order me to be a straight man. He shouldn't care, and he shouldn't have any idea that threats can shape me into someone else. There's nothing about his behavior that makes any sense. But I have to follow his weird rules or he'll cut off access to Scotty, who needs me the most. Jared and Mark I could probably still talk to on the sly.

He interrogates them, too. Like, who were you with at the basketball game, etc. I live the life he demands because I can't afford to find out what will happen if I slip up.

I HIT "SEND" before my ego could think too hard about what I'd written. Not only did I hate my father, I often hated myself for going along with his bullshit. It's just that I couldn't figure out how to stop.

Axeldental to Caxtastrophe: I'm sorry. I'm sorry that's how it is, and I'm sorry I made you talk about it. And I'm really sorry that there isn't some way we can spend time together. But at least I understand now why we can't.

Caxtastrophe to Axeldental: Ugh. Thank you. Moving on. There is one place we're going to see each other, though. At least I hope so. Intramural basketball starts next week. And the first game on the schedule is between the school of graduate studies and the athletic department.

Axeldental to Caxtastrophe: I was going to ask you about that. Is it okay if I play? Boz got me in the gym to practice last week. Seems like a fun little league.

Caxtastrophe to Axeldental: Of course it's okay if you play. What more manly venue is there than the gym? I'm counting on you being

etc.)

Axeldental to Caxtastrophe: (Insert smack talk about how you're going to lose big, etc.)

Caxtastrophe to Axeldental: Bring it, smack talker.

Axeldental to Caxtastrophe: You can bet on it.

NOTHING COULD HAVE KEPT me away from that game. Playing against Axel would probably be the highlight of my fall semester. That was pretty sad, but as with everything else in my life, there was no point in dwelling on it.

I couldn't even concentrate in the library that afternoon. I kept looking out the window, watching the sun slowly advance toward the horizon. When it was finally dark outside, I quit pretending I was studying. I packed up my stuff and headed over to the gym.

Naturally, even before the teams showed up in the gym, the outcome was predetermined. PhD candidates versus hardcore jocks? Please.

But I was eager for this drubbing. I'd lose a million to zip if it meant playing basketball with Axel one more time.

When I reached the gym, though, my eager eyes did not find Axel. Trying not to feel disappointed, I dropped my gym bag on the bleachers and peeled off my fleece jacket. Then I checked my phone one more time.

No messages.

"Can we all go out for beers after this?" asked my team-mate, Jason. He dropped his jacket onto the bench beside mine.

"Sure. Let's do it."

Jason was a few years older than I, and just the sort of laid-

he should have been ineligible for the graduate school team. At our one and only team practice last week he told me he'd graduated from the architecture program last semester. But nobody gave a damn if he wasn't a card-carrying grad student anymore. This was the most casual league ever.

Going out for beers afterward sounded like fun. I didn't have a lot of cash to throw around, but this team and the occasional night out would make my cloistered life in Henning more bearable.

"We might need more than one beer to staunch the bleeding," Jason remarked, stripping off his sweatshirt. "Looks like the athletic department picked up a new player. Don't recognize that guy from last year."

"Yeah?" My blood pressure spiked, and I gave all my attention to changing into my gym shoes.

"Oh yeah. I'm sensing our scoring chances just went down a few notches. But, hey," Jason muttered. "At least he's hot."

My pulse kicked up another notch, because now I was positive that it was Axel who'd walked in. That "hot" comment clearly described Axel.

And wasn't it funny that I'd never realized Jason was gay? My gaydar was terrible. Because it never got any practice.

I heard the familiar sound of the basketball bouncing confidently off the floor, and knowing it was Axel warming up made me feel warm everywhere. I used to love playing one-on-one together, because it allowed me to really focus on him without anyone's scrutiny. I could watch his beautiful body move, and I could get as near to him as I wanted while we fought for the ball. And nobody ever thought it was strange.

"Come on," Jason said, slapping me on the back. "Let's take our beating."

When I stood up, my eyes went immediately to Axel. The

knocked me over. I couldn't help but watch his muscular arm casually work the ball. Damn.

He lifted his chin in a subtle greeting. Then he turned his back on me and shot, sinking a perfect three-pointer.

Showoff. I buried my smile as the volunteer ref blew his whistle. "Let's go, ladies," he called. "I have a date after this."

"Well, let's not keep her waiting," growled Boz, the big ex-football player on the athletic department's team. He couldn't jump for shit, but he was big enough to get in the way at all the worst moments. He and Axel lined up for the tip-off, and I wondered how they got along at work. Boz looked like a meat-head, but Axel had told me he was a good guy. And there was something jolly about his demeanor that suggested he might not have any time for intolerance.

Not everyone in the world was a dick like my father. But growing up in his house made me mistrustful, and I didn't know if I'd ever get over that.

I was still puzzling over this when the ref tossed the ball, and Axel won the tip-off. Of course he did. He batted it to their boss—an older guy—who passed to Boz. Axel moved into position to receive the ball, so of course I lunged in to block him.

And just like that, time rolled backward.

We jockeyed for position. I leaned in, trying to cover Axel's stretch with my slightly longer but less-skilled reach. He huffed out a laugh, and I felt myself grow younger. We were fourteen again and innocent. There was nothing but the polished wooden floor, the ball, the hoop and the squeak of rubber as we vied for the ball.

Our team got the ball away from Axel, and play raced to the other end of the court. Jason passed to me, and Axel was

Finally, he fouled me as I tried to break through.

The whistle blew and we were both panting. Axel wiped sweat off his brow, his chest expanding visibly. When his eyes met mine, they sparkled with a love of the game, and a silent acknowledgment that we'd done this before.

I put my feet behind the free-throw line and sank my first shot.

"Not bad for a geek," Axel said under his breath.

Biting my lip to avoid smiling at him, I sank the second one.

The next twenty-odd minutes flew by. When the ref blew the whistle after the first half, I could hardly believe it. Walking over to my stuff, I grabbed my water bottle and took a long pull.

"You're on fire tonight," Jason said. "Seriously. Somebody ate his Wheaties today."

"It was that extra cup of coffee." But that wasn't even close to the truth. It was just so much fun to go up against Axel. I'd missed him so fucking much. My phone chirped and I picked it up.

Hey Caxtastrophe—nice hustle but you're still losing.

My reply was brief. *Hey Axeldental—bite me.*

His response: *I thought you weren't into that anymore. But you know where to find me...*

I snorted. Putting the phone down, I toweled off my forehead and went back to play. On the court was the only safe place for us to be near each other. I'd just have to enjoy every minute.

~

that much fun in a long time.

"I have to grab a shower before we go to Bruisers," Jason said.

Unbidden, my eyes flicked toward the door to the locker room. I wondered if Axel was on his way in there. The locker room was going to have to be off limits for me. "I have to stop home for a minute. Meet you at the bar?"

"Sure! I'll see if anyone from the winning team wants to join us."

"Sounds good. Give me thirty minutes." I walked outside practically humming. The world was a brighter place with Axel in it. Even if I couldn't have what I wanted, just seeing him across a room made me happy. And maybe he'd come out to the bar...

At home, I was toweling off after a quick shower when my phone rang. I didn't recognize the number. "Hello?" I answered, hoping it was a wrong number.

It wasn't.

"Hey," my brother Jared said.

"Where are you?" I asked, knowing immediately that something was wrong. Jared didn't make social calls.

"At Rob's house." The words were thick and indistinct. "Can you pick me up?"

"Of course," I said first. "Are you drunk?"

"Don't tell," he pleaded.

I was standing beside my room's door, and it made a perfect target to bang my head against. *Thunk. Thunk.* "Tell me how to find Rob's house."

Just like that, my night blew up.

After dressing hastily, I drove over to a split-level house in a residential neighborhood on the other side of town. Luckily, I didn't have to go inside to find my errant brother. He came

himself into my passenger seat. "Thanks," he mumbled.

Taking a moment to study his angular, pimple-spotted features, I tried to figure out what to say. "You want to tell me what happened?"

He groaned. "I told Dad we were studying for a test, but Rob's parents are out of town. He's like—'Let's drink the vodka, because they never touch that one.'"

"So you did it."

He stared out the window. "You pissed?"

I was careful with my answer, because I needed him to reach out to me even when he'd been stupid. "You did exactly the right thing, calling me for a ride."

He grunted.

"Is there anything else we need to do? Do you think anyone is in danger?"

Jared shook his head. "I drank the most."

"Why?"

He sighed. "They said I was chicken."

"Jared, that was..."

"Really fucking stupid. I know."

I put the car in gear. "Are you going to fall for that shit again?"

The reply was almost too low to hear. "No."

I drove us out to the diner, because I needed to sober him up before I took him home to the asshole who called himself our father. "Come on. It's a school night. Jesus. But we'll get you some pancakes and coffee. Can you eat?"

"Yeah."

He wasn't too unsteady on his feet, and he didn't look green. That was good. While I gave the waitress our order, he hid his face by looking out the window. "Were you home?" he asked eventually.

"With Amy?"

"Nope. I just had a hoops game, and we were headed out for a beer at Bruisers."

"I want your life," he said.

My laugh escaped before I thought better of it. "You do *not* want my life."

"Why?"

I shook my head. "Hey, there's something I need to tell you."

The way he turned his head toward me made it look unnaturally heavy. "What?"

"Amy and I broke up."

"Fuck." He blinked, stunned. "Why?"

"We've been together a long time, that's all." I'd been wondering what reason to give, and it sounded even lamer coming out of my mouth than it had in my head.

His eyes narrowed. "Did you cheat?"

"No! *Jesus*. Nobody cheated." It was hard to know what to say when the whole conversation was a lie. "We're still friends. She'll probably come to basketball games with us."

"Maybe you'll get back together." He looked so pathetic sitting across from me, his teen anger wrapped around him like a coat, his eyes heavy-lidded and anguished.

"Maybe," I lied. If he had to ease himself into this idea, then so be it.

My phone pinged with a text from Jason, wondering where the fuck I was. *Sorry*, I replied. *Family emergency. I hope you're not sitting there alone.*

The reply was swift. *No worries. There are six of us here. See you in the salt mines.*

I wondered who the six were, and if Axel was among them. *Sigh.*

"I'm going to call Dad," I said.

"Why?" He looked up sharply.

"Trust me. I won't throw you under the bus." I dialed, and the old grouch answered on the third ring. "Hey, Dad," I said, keeping my voice light. "I'm sitting here at the diner with Jared, and I realized it was getting late. You don't have to wait up, I'll drop him home within the hour."

There was a pause on his end of the line. "I thought he was at a friend's house."

"He was. But I wanted to see him. I had to break the news that Amy and I broke up." This was my strategy—throwing *myself* under the bus. But he was going to hear about it eventually. Probably from Scotty, who had no filter.

Two birds. One stone.

"What?" my dad snapped. "You cheat?"

Jesus Christ. My family watched too many movies. "Sorry to disappoint you, but there's no real story here." And notice that nobody said, *Hey Cax, we're sorry. This must be rough on you.*

My father gave an unintelligible grunt. "You're bringing the kid home?"

"Sure thing. After he eats his pancakes."

"All right."

I knew better than to expect a "*Thanks, Cax. You're a good brother and an asset to the family.*" "Goodnight," I said.

"G'night." *Click.*

I sighed. "Okay. Eat slowly. He'll go to bed because he knows I've got you covered. You won't even have to pretend to be sober."

Jared put an elbow on the table and lifted his eyes to mine. "Thank you."

Aw. There it was. "You're welcome. If you get into a situation, you can *always* call me." I resisted the urge to lecture him

up to bail him out. Tomorrow I could give him the lecture.

After he cleaned his plate, I drove him to the all-night pharmacy for some Advil and some breath mints, just in case our father wasn't asleep.

Then I took my brother home and told him I loved him as he got out of the car. And even though he didn't say it back, I heard it anyway.

CHAPTER TEN

Axel

Cax didn't show up at the bar that night.

I had a very pleasant time drinking with Boz and a few other guys, but it bothered me that Cax hadn't come. He'd played a hell of a ball game, and he hadn't shied away from me in the gym. Was it really too risky to share a beer in a crowded sports bar with the gay guy? Or *guys*, if we were counting Jason.

It was a fun time. Having Cax there would have made it perfect.

The next morning I emailed him from my personal account. Smack talk, of course.

Axeldental: *Well, you aren't QUITE as easy to beat at bball as you used to be.*

The reply didn't take long.

Caxtastrophe: *Thanks. I think.*

Axeldental: *This is going to sound weird. I didn't see you at the bar last night, and I just wanted to know if it was because of me. They were your friends first, so if I make you uncomfortable I can just beg off next time.*

Caxtastrophe: *You weren't the problem. I was actually on my way over to Bruisers when I got a call from my brother. He needed a*

81

drinking.

Axeldental: *Huh. Okay. So I didn't need to expose myself as both paranoid and vain? Whoops.*

Caxtastrophe: :-)

Axeldental: *Does this mean you could drink beers in a bar with me sometime?*

The reply took a while this time.

Caxtastrophe: *Probably? What am I agreeing to right now?*

Axeldental: *Here's my plan. The basketball team has an away game in Merryline this weekend. It's about a two-hour drive. After the game I'm going to a bar called The Shaft. Yes, that's the worst name for a gay bar ever. But it gets good reviews. It would be more fun if you went with me.*

After I sent that last message, I watched my phone like a hawk looking for its next meal. But there was no response for hours.

The day ticked by slowly. I wrote press releases and worked on segmenting the athletic department's mailing list by sport. And every two minutes I peered at my phone, hoping Cax would respond.

He put me out of my misery eventually.

Caxtastrophe: *So how would this little excursion work?*

I bit the inside of my cheek to keep from grinning like an idiot. Then I answered him.

Axeldental: *I'll ride the team's bus out to Merryline. But I booked myself into a different hotel, because I like my privacy. After the game, I'll take a cab to the bar. You'd have to drive up. It's about ninety miles. But you can crash in my hotel room if you want.*

I won't lie—I rewrote the message a few more times, trying to make it sound casual. It took me a while to hit send. I hated rejection as much as the next guy. But if you don't ask, you can't ever hear "yes."

Treadmills weren't my thing, but there was snow on the ground pretty much all the time now. So I found the college's indoor track and pounded out four miles listening to hip-hop on my iPod. When I got home, I found three emails in succession.

Caxtastrophe: *You're looking for loopholes again. I don't get to have loopholes.*

Caxtastrophe: *I don't know a soul in Merryline, though.*

Caxtastrophe: *What does a guy wear to a place called The Shaft? I'm picturing leather pants and a dog collar.*

The last message made me howl with laughter as I tried to picture conservatively dressed Cax in leather.

Axeldental: *I'm wearing jeans and a T-shirt. I figure the collar is optional.*

∾

THERE WERE NO MORE messages that night and none the next day.

Was there any chance he was coming to Merryline? Probably not. I convinced myself that it was crazy to ask him. But hope springs eternal. So I put condoms and lube in the interior pocket of my overnight bag. And I brought a nice shirt to wear out to the bar. I told myself that it was worth it, anyway. I was going to a gay bar for the first time in months. I might as well look good.

I put Cax out of my mind when I boarded the team bus on Friday. There was too much basketball mojo in the air to stress about it, anyway. I listened to the coach's speech, and I listened to the players psyching themselves up. And I tried to appreciate the parts of my life that were going well.

Lonely was a state of mind, after all. And I wasn't going to choose it tonight.

CHAPTER ELEVEN

Caxton

I had no idea how I'd come to point my car toward Merryline, Massachusetts. That's what I'd been telling myself, anyway.

Earlier I'd asked Amy if she wanted to see a movie. It was the first time I'd asked her to hang out since she'd told me about her I.T. boyfriend. But they had plans together. Of course they did.

I'd been so desperate not to be at loose ends that I'd asked each of my three brothers to the movies. I was even prepared to see a kid flick with Scotty. That's how desperate I was. But to a man, they were busy. Even Scotty, who had a sleepover birthday party.

It was like God had ordered me to drive to Merryline to be with Axel.

I'd thrown a change of clothes and a toothbrush into my duffel bag, and, as the GPS directed me out of town, I said a silent prayer that none of my brothers would end up needing me tonight. It would be just my kind of luck for someone to have a crisis when I was ninety miles away.

Still, I went. This adventure felt like a stolen opportunity. Nobody knew where I was going, not even the man I was

in Merryline, a posh suburb where rich Bostonians moved to have larger yards.

It was incredibly liberating to walk out of my life for a night.

Then there was the matter of the gay bar. When Axel had written me that he was going, my first reaction was, *I could never go to a place like that*. But after I thought about it for a while, I pictured Axel going there alone. And then I pictured Axel getting hit on by half the men in the bar. That bothered the shit out of me, because I knew it would happen.

Of course, my traitorous brain moved the daydream right along—to Axel leaving with a guy. Axel making out with him on a hotel bed. Axel's clothes coming off...

That image was what finally gave me enough incentive to cast aside my fears and get into the car.

It was a long and winding road eastward toward the Boston 'burbs. When I got close, I stopped my car to gas up, and while fuel filled my tank I emailed Axel. He'd check the email account, wouldn't he? Unless he'd written me off already.

Caxtastrophe: *Where are you? I'm about ten minutes from the bar.*

I got my answer before the pump clicked off.

Axeldental: *Changing to go out. Pick me up at the Merryline Motor Lodge?*

He didn't express any shock that I was here. I didn't know whether to be annoyed or grateful.

To the confusion of my GPS device, I detoured to his motel. When I pulled in, I realized I didn't know how to find him. But the second time I scanned the row of motel room doors, I saw Axel jogging toward my car.

He opened the door and slid into the passenger seat. "Hey," he said. As if we did this all the time.

He beamed at me, those chocolate eyes twinkling. The smile he gave me went straight to my dick. "Of course you're not. But we're doing this anyway."

"Really? You want to go to a place called The Shaft?"

He pointed out the windshield. "Drive, Cax. We have to see the place, if only for the entertainment value. Let's go."

So I drove. It was only a couple of miles away, and when I pulled into the parking lot, the female voice of my GPS announced the success. "You have arrived at...The Shaft!"

We burst out laughing. And it felt damned good.

I followed Axel into a cavernous, crowded room. Men were three deep at the bar. There were tables all around the edges of the place and pool tables in the far corner.

Axel spoke into my ear, because it was so loud I wouldn't hear him otherwise. "I'm going to fight my way over to the bar for some drinks. You want a glass of cabernet?"

I shook my head. "Beer. Whatever you're drinking." I reached for my wallet, but he put his hand on mine. "I got this. Be right back."

He walked off and I let my eyes roam, trying to take it all in. Men with men, as far as the eye could see. I'd always wondered what freedom looked like. And now I knew—it looked like this place. There were a few women here and there, but they were the exception. Mostly I saw men in pairs, their heads together—talking, laughing. *Kissing.* I tried not to stare, but their openness was an education for me.

My eye kept snagging on one couple in particular—two guys in their twenties. Each of them held a bottle of beer in one hand and the other man's bicep in the other. They were pressing kiss after open-mouthed kiss against one another. Like long lost lovers.

And now I was hard and feeling guilty for staring.

somewhere quieter," he said, pointing his chin toward the back. I followed him to a recently abandoned high table, empty glasses still cluttering it.

A bus boy wearing painted-on jeans and a wifebeater hustled over to clear it for us. "Thanks," I said before sitting down on one of the bar stools.

"No dance floor. Bummer," Axel said, pushing two beers in my direction. Then he laughed. "You should have seen the look on your face when I said 'dance floor.'"

"I don't dance."

He grinned. "We'll work up to it."

We wouldn't, though. There weren't going to be more nights like this. I didn't get to walk away from my life very often, and even now I worried that my phone would vibrate in my pocket with some new disaster, and the gig would be up. So I took a long pull of the excellent ale that Axel had chosen and let my eyes drift around the room. "Let me ask you a question."

"Shoot."

"If I didn't come here with you tonight, what's your usual play? Would you just find somebody to hook up with?" I'd never had the chance to indulge in the life I wanted. But even if nobody cared what I did, I wasn't sure how I'd fit in with the hookup scene. The idea of getting naked with a stranger I'd met in a bar was intimidating.

The smile slid off his face. "Well, I like coming to these places, and there's always somebody on the prowl."

I didn't doubt it. Anyone would take one look at Axel and buy him a drink. He was the whole package—gorgeous body, cute face. Clever. Fun. Exactly the guy I'd want if I could date a man.

"But I don't do many bar hookups. It's risky." His eyes did a

before where I felt unsafe. It's not the kind of thing you want to repeat."

"I'll bet."

He returned his gaze to me. "So if I came here alone tonight, I'd probably play some pool." He tipped his head toward the tables in the corner. "But at the end of the night, I'd probably leave alone. Unless there was some super chill, charming guy who made me feel both safe and excited. *And* he looked like a cross between Zac Efron and Channing Tatum."

I laughed. "Good luck with that."

He leaned one of his gorgeous cheekbones into his palm and smiled at me. "That's how I think of you, though."

I swallowed my surprise behind a gulp of beer. "That's a bit of a stretch, my friend. I think the ref is going to argue that call."

He didn't say anything more. There was only his smile, which I felt in my groin, and the heat in his eyes. *Christ.* I hadn't let myself think about how this night might end. My plan was to stay sober enough to drive back to Henning. But I knew that Axel had different ideas about tonight. And I'd packed a bag, just in case...

"What are you thinking about?" he asked.

"Nothing. Want to shoot some pool?"

His smile was teasing. "Sure. But don't be too upset if I crush you like a bug."

"We'll just see about that."

I BEAT him the first two games. But then my attention wavered, because every time I leaned across the table, I felt Axel's dark eyes on me. And every time he brushed past me to

too, that fucker. He began putting a hand on my back from time to time. His touch was casual, but my body didn't care. I wanted more, and concentrating on the game became all but impossible.

Every sensation tonight was so new. The music pulsed through my limbs and hips, feeding the electric charge I felt in my veins. I was having fun, and I was turned on and kind of nervous. My body hummed with an unfamiliar electricity.

So this was what living your life felt like.

"You want to get out of here?" Axel said after he sank the 8-ball on our third game. He leaned against the table's edge, and his pecs flexed while my mouth watered.

"Sure." More nerves sizzled through my chest. We hadn't discussed what would happen now.

Axel's eyes flashed. He set down his cue, then removed mine from my hand. Then? He put his hand on my ass. "Let's go." His voice was rough.

I was tongue-tied as I followed him outside. We got into my car, and I actually dropped my keys on the floor because my hands were sweating.

"Hey," Axel said, lifting a hand to my arm. "You okay?"

"Yeah." I shoved the key in the ignition, but his hand didn't move. Even though I knew my nerves would show on my face, I turned slowly to look at him.

Axel licked his lips. "Are you coming back to the hotel with me tonight? I asked the hotel for a room with two beds, because I would never pressure you. But I don't think you should drive all the way back to Henning now. It's late."

My stomach quivered, because I knew what would happen if I went inside that room with him. "Okay." I started the engine and left the bar's parking lot, careful to keep all my focus on the road. The ride back to his motel took a ridicu-

wheel as I pulled into a parking space. I snapped the keys out of the ignition and turned to reach for my duffel in back.

But Axel stopped me with a hand on my thigh. "Cax?"

"Hmm?" I breathed, suddenly all too aware of how close he was to me, and where we were. At a freaking *motel*.

He gave my leg a squeeze, and I almost died from yearning. "I need to know what to expect. Before we go into that room, you need to tell me if we're hooking up or not. If you just need a place to crash, I'm fine with that. But don't make me guess your thoughts."

I let out an achy breath. But I didn't say a word. Instead, I put my hand over his and squeezed.

Axel flipped his hand over to grasp mine. His thumb caressed my palm, and *holy hell*. I had no idea there were so many nerve endings in my hand. "I still need to hear you say it," he whispered. "You're not so easy to read."

"I want to," I whispered.

"You want to what?" he returned. "If you can't say it, we shouldn't do it. I care about you, Cax. You make me crazy, but I don't want to get this wrong."

Oh, the agony. He wasn't going to let me be my usual chicken-shit self. I took a deep breath. "I want to hook up."

"Are you going to regret it later?" Axel asked gently.

"No." I gave my head a firm shake. "I've always wanted you. And this might be our only chance."

He picked up my hand and brought it up to his mouth. The kiss he planted on my palm was gentle and arousing all at once. "Then let's go," he whispered.

I grabbed my duffel and got out of that car faster than you can say "desperate."

He didn't make me wait. As soon as he got the door open, we ducked inside. He kicked the door shut and then pushed

91

body lined up to mine, and his kiss found my mouth in the dark.

Warm, firm lips caressed me. I opened for him, ready to taste him on my tongue. He moaned against my mouth, and then met me in a wild kiss. Jesus, I was on fire. And so was he. Ten seconds in, we were making out like porn stars, his hips pinning mine to the door. I wasn't the only one who was hard inside my jeans. I was trapped between two hard objects and I freaking loved it. There were no decisions to make. My only choice was to lean in and enjoy him. Every stroke of his tongue convinced me that I'd made the right call.

A strong hand cupped my jaw, tilting my head for a better angle. "Been waiting..." he said between kisses. "...my whole life to get you naked."

"You don't have to wait anymore." It wasn't the most original line, but I liked delivering it. Just for tonight I could be that guy—the one who drinks at a gay bar and has sex in a hotel room.

And with Axel Armitage, who I'd wanted my whole life.

The next kiss was so hot that I felt my balls tighten. Jesus Christ, I could come in my jeans just from making out like this. I turned my head, breaking the kiss so that I could calm down for a second. Eager hands worked open the buttons of my shirt. I took a few deep breaths and let him do all the work.

I rested my shaking hands on his hips. The feel of his solid body made me want to shout with excitement. I could hardly believe that I was really here, and we were going to get busy. I dug my fingers into the fabric of his shirt, and tugged it out of his jeans. Then, in a move that felt impossibly bold, but I put a hand under his shirt to palm his firm stomach. *Yesss*. These were the abs that had tortured me from beneath his tight-

beneath his smooth skin felt every bit as good as I'd imagined.

Axel popped the button on my jeans, and my heart skipped a beat or four. I was a cocktail of fear and excitement. With shaking hands, I reached down and undid his belt, while Axel unbuttoned his own shirt. "What do you like?" he asked me.

I'd never lived one of my fantasies before. I didn't answer his question, because I liked *everything* that was happening here. With his belt out of the way, I unzipped his jeans. A whimper may or may not have escaped my lips as my fingertips brushed the hard cock straining against his underwear.

Axel kicked off his shoes and jeans in a flash. Then he grabbed my hand and pulled me through the darkened room until we both scrambled onto a bed. He tried to yank off my jeans, but it took a second until I worked out that I needed to help him. When they were gone, I threw my socks overboard. That left me in an unbuttoned shirt and boxer briefs.

By the time Axel rolled on top of me a few seconds later, he was gloriously naked. I wrapped my arms around him and squeezed. My hands took a trip down his bare back, gliding over miles of warm skin, coasting onto his bare, muscular ass... I shuddered from excitement.

He kissed me once. Twice. "Caxy, talk to me. I have supplies if you want to fuck. I'm verse, but it's been a long time since I bottomed. You'll have to warm me up if we're doing that."

I groaned. The idea of fucking Axel was almost too much.

He kissed me again. "Is that what you want?"

Probably not, actually. Because I didn't have any experience, except for watching porn. And I'd *die* if I did it wrong and hurt him. "I'm too impatient," I said, and that was one hundred percent true. If he kept kissing me and grinding on me, I was going to burst before this conversation was over.

come." As he said it, he slipped a hand down the front of my briefs and grabbed my dick. My bellow echoed off the walls. "Fuck, you're so hard." He squeezed the base of my dick. "Don't come yet, though."

"Easy for you to say."

He laughed. When he slid off my body and left the bed, I got a chance to relax for a second. I shucked off my underwear and my shirt, wondering what would happen next. I felt exposed, lying naked on the bed of a motel room. I may have had jitters, but I wasn't actually afraid. Axel would never hurt me.

No matter how many lonely years were between us, I trusted him implicitly.

When he came back to the bed, I heard the quiet snap of a lube bottle. Goosebumps broke out on my skin. In the light of the digital clock beside the bed, I saw him set the lube down. Then he reached between my legs and palmed my balls with slicked fingers.

"Aaah," I gasped.

He bent over my chest, planting a kiss on my sternum. "If I do something you don't like, just tell me to stop, okay?"

I put my hand in his hair to tell him that I understood. But speech was impossible, because he'd begun to lick his way down my chest and onto my quivering stomach. I shuddered and gasped as his mouth headed toward my needy dick. And when his lips finally skimmed my tip, we both moaned.

"Fuck, you're leaking for me," he whispered. "Sexiest thing ever."

His warm, wet mouth sank onto my dick, and I wasn't going to survive it. I made sounds I'd never made before. I'd dreamed about this so many times, but the real-life experience was so much more powerful than I'd expected. My fantasies

94

stubble against my inner thighs. The friction of skin against skin.

The flat of his tongue running down my shaft made every one of my muscles tighten. Then he swirled his tongue around my cockhead, and I thought I would lose my mind.

He eased off my cock, and I thought he was giving me another moment to calm down. But naughty, slicked-up fingers stroked my taint, and it felt gloriously naughty. And then Axel lifted my knee, opening me up. His finger slid back and began teasing my hole.

My gasp was as loud as a hurricane gale.

He backed off immediately. "Sorry," he whispered.

"No, I..." My chest rose and fell as if I'd just run a sprint. "Caught off guard," I ground out.

"Relax," he whispered, stroking my taint with two fingers. "I want to take care of you."

"Shouldn't take much effort."

Chuckling, he reached for the lube again, and I heard the click of the cap. I was trembling by the time his slicked fingers stroked into my crease again. This time when his finger pressed my hole, I managed not to freak out. But I didn't forget my self-consciousness until he bent over me again and swallowed my dick *all the way to the back of his throat*. My fingers gripped the bedspread. He gave a good, hard suck and I couldn't hold in my moan.

Nothing had *ever* felt this good. I couldn't hold my hips still, so they began to roll in a rhythm with Axel's mouth. Meanwhile, the finger against my ass pressed onward. He was penetrating me, and I wasn't even shocked anymore. I was too busy fucking his mouth and seeing spots in front of my eyes.

Then his finger stroked me inside, and I gasped again. My balls tightened and it was all over. I didn't have time to warn

crazy.

Axel groaned, swallowing again and again, taking everything I gave him. Then he gentled his mouth, easing off me, kissing me once more on the tip. He withdrew his finger from my ass, and I gasped at the loss of him.

He kissed my hip and my belly. "Christ. You are so... Just don't go anywhere."

Axel disappeared for a minute into the bathroom, and I heard the sink running while he probably washed his hands. I slowed my panting breaths and put a hand over my eyes to shield them from the bathroom light.

When Axel came back, he pulled the hand off my face. "You okay?"

"I have never felt better." I reached for him, and he slipped into my arms, his hard dick poking me in the hip. Soft lips grazed my shoulder and I sighed. "Think it's your turn," I said, slipping a hand down onto his cock—the only one I'd ever touched that wasn't mine. Just like it had been when we were teens, touching him was strange and familiar all at once. I pumped my hand up and down his shaft—we were about the same size, actually.

That had to be the only benefit of celibacy—I'd never had to worry about comparing my dick to anyone else's.

Axel was so quiet that I looked up at his face. The light was dim, but I could see he was staring at me.

"What?" I asked.

He smiled slowly. "Just can't believe I'm here with you. Blowing you was so hot I almost came myself."

I swiped my thumb through the pre-come on his cockhead, and his breath hitched. "I want to make this good for you," I said. *But I don't know what I'm doing.* "Maybe you should fuck me."

like to bottom?"

I hesitated, because I didn't want to lie. "For you I'd like to." I stroked him a little faster. He was so hard in my hand.

Axel closed his hand over mine. "Baby, hang on." Concerned eyes met mine. "Have you bottomed before?"

Slowly, I shook my head.

He bit one of his full, gorgeous lips. "So you usually top?"

This was not the conversation I wanted to have. "There is no *usually*."

"I get that. But..." He frowned. "Have you never done this at all?" Another shake of my head, and his eyes got wide. "Oh Cax, *really?*" He put a hand over my heart and looked into my eyes.

Great. I'd just ruined the mood. "It's not that I don't want to."

Axel's expression went soft. He put his cheek down on my chest. "When's the last time you fooled around with a guy?"

"It was with you," I whispered.

His whole body went still. "Not in college?"

Embarrassed, I shook my head. "Too risky."

"That's the saddest thing I ever heard."

I sighed. "I know I'm pathetic. Can we stop talking about it now?"

Warm, lovely hands began to caress my chest. "Babe, I didn't mean to make you feel bad. But there's no way I'm fucking you tonight."

"*Why?* This could be our only chance."

He lifted his head to look into my eyes. "Don't say that. You're twenty-two years old, Cax. There are years of excellent fucking in your future."

But not with you. I knew this was a one-time thing. Axel wouldn't want to wait around for me to get out of my shitty

97

him or how flattered I was that he wanted me. Wanting wasn't enough to make it work.

"We're here now, though," I reminded both of us. "You have to make hay while the sun shines."

He gave me a slow kiss. "I didn't say we had to stop. But we'll save fucking for another time. There's no rush."

My body disagreed. Even though I'd had an explosive orgasm a few minutes before, my dick perked right up again when Axel rolled on top of me. His kisses were slow and smoldering, and his gorgeous dick lined up beside mine. Every bump and scrape made me hotter.

"Mmm," he sighed into my mouth. He rolled his hips, and it was delicious. "I could come like this," he whispered between kisses.

"Do it," I groaned. "Shoot on me."

He thrust against me, shuddering. "Where?" he breathed.

Reaching around him, I palmed his ass and squeezed. "Everywhere. Come all over me." I'd never said something so dirty in my life. But it was shockingly easy to say exactly what you wanted when you trusted someone so completely.

Panting, he sat up, his ass on my thighs. He wrapped a hand around his cock, but I knocked it away. With a firm grip, I jacked him. He dropped his chin to watch me, his six-pack heaving, his sculpted arms tensed into fists. With a slow, insistent rhythm, I pumped my hand along his cock. After a minute he made a guttural noise, and then I felt the first splash of come on my stomach. The sight of Axel climaxing was so beautiful. I could have watched him forever, but he dropped forward into the mess on my chest and kissed me. "Fuck. I'm dizzy."

I put my arms around him before I could think better of the idea. "Is this okay?"

"Never hooked up with a guy before. Don't know what to do afterward."

He nuzzled my jaw. "Cuddling and a shower. Then you're supposed to give me a thirty minute back massage..."

I pinched Axel's ass and he laughed. His laughter turned into kisses on my neck, and I'd never felt so much joy.

My eyes stung from happiness, and I was grateful to the darkness for hiding the fact that I was such a sap.

$\sim$

THERE *WAS* CUDDLING AND A SHOWER. We washed each other's hair, and it was almost more intimate than getting a blowjob. The lights were on, which meant that I was staring into Axel's brown eyes as I shampooed him.

We both got all boned up again, of course. So Axel poured another dollop of shampoo into his hand and jacked us together while we kissed. I came with his tongue in my mouth and my hands on his ass, and he followed immediately. We were still breathing hard when I put my lips beside his ear. "Love watching you come."

His hand gripped my waist. "Back at you, hon."

When we got out of the shower, my body felt impossibly warm and sated. I chased drops of water off my skin with a towel, then stumbled into my underwear.

Axel brushed his teeth and climbed into bed before I did. When I emerged from the bathroom, I didn't know what to do. I walked slowly around the room, into the space between the two beds. I wanted to climb in with Axel, but I didn't know what he expected of me. Setting my watch on the nightstand, I was still puzzling over it when Axel flipped the covers aside, making room for me.

but apparently that wasn't good enough, because he tugged me halfway onto his chest. I settled onto his pillow, my face in the crook of his neck. He smelled like hotel soap and pure man.

"Been waiting a long time for this, too," he murmured.

"Mmm." I didn't know what to say. This would be the first time in my life I'd ever slept with a lover. (Amy and I had shared a bed on vacation, but it was well after our ridiculously brief sexual relationship. It in no way counted.)

The fact that I was in Axel's arms? It was an unexpected gift. I was determined to appreciate it, even if I knew I only got one night.

"You know…" He hesitated.

"What?"

"This should seem…unfamiliar. We haven't seen each other for years. We've never done *this*. But it's…nice. Familiar. Not weird." He sighed. "Am I crazy?"

I shook my head, too overcome to speak much. "You're still you." It might be the dumbest sentence I'd ever uttered. But that's exactly how I felt. The Axel I'd always wanted was the same one who lay here with me. My memory of him hadn't lied to me.

"You're still you, too," he whispered. Then he kissed me on the top of the head and it made me ridiculously happy.

CHAPTER TWELVE

Axel

I woke up pressed up against Cax, his hard dick poking me in the ass. A little morning sex would have been fun, but the hotel clock showed that it was already eight o'clock. The team bus was leaving at eight-thirty, and I had to be on it.

Sliding out of bed, I was careful not to wake him. He looked so peaceful—his sandy hair against the pillow, his face serene.

Tiptoeing into the bathroom, I considered asking him for a ride back to Henning. But then I'd have to explain to the team that I'd caught a ride, which would sound odd. And I knew I'd already pushed Cax with this stolen getaway. He wouldn't really want anyone to see him dropping me off in town. I didn't want to ask that of him.

After I got dressed and brushed my teeth, I found Cax stirring in the bed.

"You can sleep," I said. "But my bus is leaving soon."

He raised his head. "How will you get there?"

"I think I'll walk. It's just a few blocks."

He slid his legs over the side of the bed. "I'll drop you."

THERE WASN'T any time for awkwardness. We jumped into our clothes, packed, and then shoved our bags into his car.

In the parking lot of the team's hotel, Cax picked a spot that was well away from the waiting bus. As he put the car into park, we saw athletes in Barmuth jackets emerging from the front door.

"Thanks for the lift," I said, trying for casual.

He sighed. "Thanks for *everything*." His hazel eyes flickered to mine and then away again. "I had a great time."

I slid a hand onto his leg. "So did I. If you have any ideas about how we can do it again, I'm all ears. The next away game is two weeks from now in Providence."

"Which night?" he asked softly.

"The tenth."

Cax leaned back, his head bumping the headrest. "That's the night of Scotty's holiday concert."

"So...you have to go to that?"

He turned his head. "I'm the only one who shows up at these things. I know it doesn't sound like a big deal but..."

I held up a hand. "I get it. It's part of the bigger picture."

"For four years I let him twist so I could get away from my father's bullshit. But my brothers can't escape yet. So I'm there to make it better. I'm trying to show my face as often as I can, so if something goes bad at home they know exactly who to call."

He was a bigger man than I was. "They're so lucky to have you. I hope you know that."

Cax squeezed my hand. "God, Axel. You're killing me. I hate saying no to you when I really want to say yes."

I wrapped my fingers around his. *Don't be sad*. The words were on the tip of my tongue, but this time I didn't say them. I

broken. No matter how much I wanted to.

"I know it's a drag," he said with a sigh. "Thank you for changing my life for a single night."

"Anytime." I meant that literally. "I really want to kiss you right now," I said honestly.

He eyed the activity near the bus. "That's a bad idea."

I don't think so. "I'll see you at the gym, maybe?"

"Sure."

There was no more to say, so I got out of the car and boarded the bus.

~

Axeldental to Caxtastrophe: *My bball team is playing the engineering school tomorrow night. Should I be afraid?*

Caxtastrophe to Axeldental: *You're kidding, right? They play in black socks. Just watch out for their glasses.*

Axeldental to Caxtastrophe: *You have a game too?*

Caxtastrophe to Axeldental: *Not tomorrow. Our next one is Tuesday, vs. the medical school. They are surprisingly good. It's all that ambition and ego.*

Axeldental to Caxtastrophe: *Thanks for the heads up. My game against the engineers is at six. Beers at Bruisers after?*

Caxtastrophe to Axeldental: *Can't. Got too much work to do after blowing off the weekend.*

Axeldental to Caxtastrophe: *Mmm... blowing. So good.*

Caxtastrophe to Axeldental: *And now I'm hard in the library.*

Axeldental to Caxtastrophe: *Not my problem. Unless you want it to be. Later!*

CHAPTER THIRTEEN

Caxton

"Hey!" Jason squeezed my shoulder at the library the next afternoon. "Can I buy you a beer after you're finished here? There's something I need to talk to you about."

"Um... I'm good for strictly one beer. Then I have some more work to plow through." If Axel had heard me say that, there would probably be a "plow" joke coming my way.

I really needed to stop thinking about Axel.

"Good enough," Jason said, tapping my stack of books with his phone. "I'll grab you at six?"

"Thanks."

BRUISERS WAS QUIET TONIGHT. Jason and I took seats at the bar and settled in over longnecks.

"The Celtics don't look as bad as this year as usual," he said, toying with the paper coaster under his beer bottle. "If I buy this house I'm looking at in Merryline, I can probably see some games next year."

"Merryline?" I said, perking up. The name of that town

the remainder of my natural life.

"Yeah, if I want to find any decent clients I need to be in a more wealthy area. I already found an office space. But I can't commute ninety minutes to work every day."

"So you're buying a house?" I couldn't imagine having enough money to do that. It was my dream.

"Yup. A fixer-upper. It's probably too big for me. I'm going to rattle around in there."

"You can install a giant TV for your Celtics."

He laughed. "You don't like the Celts?"

"Eh. The Bulls are my team."

"You never told me how you came to root for Chicago."

Because of Axel. "Because I grew up in Ohio, I guess. So it would have been the Bulls or the Cavs. We moved here when I was in high school." My eyes did a sweep of the room, and it was then that I remembered I'd told Axel I couldn't go out for a beer tonight. Sipping my Long Trail Ale, I tried not to feel like too big of an asshole.

I *did* have work to do tonight—that was absolutely true— but that wasn't why I'd turned him down. I didn't think I could sit across from him in public and act casual.

Even before we'd been naked together, I got hot just looking at him. But since our night together I'd turned into a raging hormone. I'd spent hours reliving every one of our moments together. The sounds he made when he came. The taste of his mouth and the feel of his shower-slicked skin under my hands.

I couldn't sit across from him drinking a beer and talking about the NBA or what-the-fuck-ever. My eyes would wander onto his crotch, his lips, his hands... I might as well wear a T-shirt reading: *Flaming and Infatuated*.

But it was only 6:15. Axel would be playing the engineers

drinking began, I'd be at home reading like I said I was going to do.

"So, there's something I need to ask you," Jason said.

"Shoot."

"That guy Axel on the athletic department team—you know him?"

I felt a prickle of sweat on my back. Where was this coming from? "A little." I took a gulp of my beer to hide my confusion.

"He's gay, right?"

I actually choked on the beer. My face probably turned bright red as I coughed into the crook of my arm. I had no idea why he'd ask me this. Jason watched me, his face impassive, waiting for my answer. "Why do you ask?" I finally gritted out.

Jason's eyes widened. "Because he's cute and I want to ask him out. But I won't do that if he's straight..." He frowned at me. "Or if I'm stepping on your toes."

My brain practically exploded. "What? No. You're not..." *Really?* Jason? *And what had he just implied about me?*

"I'm not what?" Jason's eyes narrowed. "Gay?"

Shit. He'd surprised me, and everything I was saying was coming out wrong. "Stepping on my *toes*," I said, still trying not to cough. "That's what I meant."

His face softened. "Are you sure? I mean, you are gay, right?"

"Why would you think that?" Panic rose in my chest, and not just because Jason had somehow figured me out. It was starting to sink in that Jason wanted to date Axel. *Jesus Christ.* If they became a thing, I'd have to stand by and pretend I didn't care.

Jason blinked at me. "Well, this conversation got awkward

frustrated breath.

"It's... Let's just forget about it," I said, still panicking. Still trying to cover my ass. "Actually, I have to go." I took one more gulp of my beer and threw a ten down on the bar.

He squinted at me. "Already?"

"Got shit to do," I said. I knew I was acting like a freak, but I had to get out of there. Yanking my coat off the back of the barstool, I headed for the door.

I made it as far as the parking lot before the evening got even worse. I was two steps out the door when a voice called out. "Dude!"

It was Boz from the athletic department. "The engineers forfeited!" he howled. "Those pussies. Couldn't field a team."

I looked past him and found Axel watching me with a frown on his face. "You're leaving?" he asked.

"Got work to do," I said. "Have fun." It came out sounding bitter, even though Axel had done nothing wrong. But Jason would still be sitting at the bar, and I'd just given him the all-clear to ask Axel out.

Fuck my life.

I stalked past them both and kept on walking.

CHAPTER FOURTEEN

Axel

I followed Boz into the bar, trying not to wear a kicked-puppy expression. My coworker kept yammering about the engineers and how lame it was that they were too busy with their calculators to find five guys to shoot some hoops. I didn't respond. I was too busy wondering why Cax had time to drink a beer after work, but not with me.

His teammate Jason sat at the bar watching a sports highlight reel on the television. Beside him sat a half-empty bottle of beer that I'm pretty sure must have been Cax's.

Cax liked the sex, but he won't even be seen in public with you, a little voice in my head complained.

He was afraid—I understood that. But I wasn't asking Cax to hold hands while we walked through the center of campus. I just thought we could have a beer together, like all the straight dudes in the bar.

"You eating?" Boz asked, waving at the bartender. "I feel a cheeseburger coming on."

"Sure. Order two." I hadn't spent much money this week. I could afford a burger and fries.

started scribbling on his order pad.

Jason flashed me a smile. "Have a seat. This one was just vacated."

"Yeah? Thanks." I pointed at a third stool for Boz, but he held up a finger and wandered off to talk to someone else he knew.

I sat down beside Jason. "Hi again."

"No game with the pocket-protector crew, huh? We play the med school next."

"I heard they're good."

"Surprisingly good. All those ambitious guys who want to play God? They have sharp elbows on the court."

"I'll keep that in mind when we play them."

"Can I buy you a drink?" Jason asked.

That woke me up. I turned to find him giving me a shy smile. "Um, thanks? Just, uh, a beer would be great."

He waved to the bartender, and I wondered if the offer of a drink was just a friendly thing, or a precursor to a different kind of offer.

I tried on that idea while the bartender fetched my beer. At any other time in my life, a hookup with a sexy, slightly older guy would be a rare and precious offer. I studied Jason, thinking it over. He was really handsome. Wavy hair, blonder than Cax's. Great bone structure. Gorgeous blue eyes. He was goddamned pretty, really.

And I didn't feel a thing.

A beer bottle landed in front of me, and I took it. "Cheers," I said, lifting my bottle to his.

"Cheers. And before Boz comes back, I have a question." I looked into those baby blues and braced myself. "This isn't easy, because I never do this. Like *never*." He chuckled. "But can we have dinner sometime?"

exchange blowjobs. He was cute *and* classy enough to offer a real date? Pinch me. And how often did a nice, available gay man ask me out?

Not often. Not often at *all*.

But he wasn't Cax.

"I..." I heard myself stammering. "I would like to say yes. But it's complicated."

His smile dimmed by only a fraction. "I see."

Pushing a hand through my hair, I tried to maintain eye contact. I wanted him to know that it wasn't about him. "Can't believe I'm saying this, because I'm *never* complicated. But there's someone I'm kind of hung up on."

"Ah." He smiled again, and it was friendly. "Well, keep me in mind, in case you become less complicated. I did notice that the Celtics are playing the Bulls at home next month. Even if we're just friends, I thought you might like to come with me."

"Oh, man." I rubbed my face, which was turning redder. "You don't fight fair."

He laughed. "I was trying to say that we should be friends anyway. You're new in town. And we could go to a basketball game no matter what."

"That is a hell of an offer. Sounds like a blast," I said truthfully.

Jason sipped his beer. "This is a small town. You can't have too many friends who like both basketball and dick."

With a snort, I touched my bottle to his once more. "Good point, my friend. Good point."

Caxtastrophe to Axeldental: *I'm sorry I didn't stay for a beer last night. It's not you.*

Wait—scratch that. That was a shitty reply. I'm just frustrated. In all the ways there are to be frustrated. ;)

Caxtastrophe to Axeldental: *I'm... yeah. But I DO say that a lot. It's just that I don't see that changing any time soon. My life is a suck-fest, and not the enjoyable kind.*

Axeldental to Caxtastrophe: *And now I'm thinking about BJs. Thanks for that.*

Caxtastrophe to Axeldental: *You're welcome. Frustrating you is my specialty. But I mean well.*

Axeldental to Caxtastrophe: *I know you do. But I don't have to like it. Last night I turned down a date.*

Caxtastrophe to Axeldental: *You did? Why?*

Axeldental to Caxtastrophe: *Because he wasn't you.*

Caxtastrophe to Axeldental: *Maybe you shouldn't have done that.*

I GROANED.

"What?" Boz asked, chomping on his gum.

"Nothing." I'd been grumpy all day. The emails from Cax weren't helping.

Boz pushed back from his desk and then spun his office chair. "You're in a mood. I'd ask you if you were having woman troubles but..."

"It's possible to have man troubles, you know."

"I suppose. But I refuse to believe that guys are tough to get along with. I mean...it's tempting to go gay just to get away from female drama."

I laughed for the first time all day. "Not sure you're right about that. But it would be an interesting experiment. Can I watch?"

Boz crumpled up a piece of paper and threw it at me.

He spun the chair again, and I was getting dizzy just watching. "So, whoever he is—just go talk to him. Bring beer. Play a gory video game. Problem solved."

"If only it were that simple."

"It probably is, though. *I'm* that simple, anyway."

"Let's not print that on your business cards."

Boz laughed. "You really know what to say to a guy. You want to show me the work you've done on the subscribers' list before the day is over?"

"Sure."

I DIDN'T GET any emails from Cax the following day. That made me grumpy.

The next night found me bumping around my apartment, alone again. It was December, so the sun had set at five o'clock. It was dark and cold, and my mood was bleak.

My gaze kept landing on the Barmuth sweatshirt hanging by my door. It belonged to Cax and I still hadn't returned it. Thinking it was mine, I'd grabbed it off the backseat of his car when he'd dropped me off at the team hotel in Merryline.

And *maybe* in a weak moment I *might* have given it a little sniff, to see if it smelled like him.

It did. And that only made me miss him more.

What's worse, I was pining for someone who'd never been, and who never could be, really mine. Maybe I was some kind of masochist to keep thinking about him, but we had so much potential as a couple. The chemistry between us was off the charts. And we'd been friends since we were *eight*. When I was sixteen, I'd realized I loved him.

I still loved him. Not that Cax wanted to hear it.

his face, if only for a minute.

I put it in my backpack when I walked to work the following morning. As I sat at my desk, thinking about taking it to him on a break or at lunch, I began to wonder if Cax would want me near his apartment building. He was so worried about the world knowing who he really was…

Fuck. Could he not even have a gay friend without casting suspicion on himself?

Axeldental to Caxtastrophe: *I happen to have your Barmuth sweatshirt.*
Caxtastrophe to Axeldental: *I wondered where that went.*
Axeldental to Caxtastrophe: *Okay if I drop by later and return it?*

There was a pause before he answered, and it made me feel like a pariah.

Caxtastrophe to Axeldental: *You can swing by, but I might be out running.*
Axeldental to Caxtastrophe: *Fine. If you're not there I'll leave it in a bag at your door.*

I had to stop brooding over him. It was only going to make me crazier than I already was.

That afternoon I left work at two o'clock, because I had a few hours coming to me on account of the basketball schedule. Cax had told me where he lived, and I'd written down the address. Still, it took the new guy in town a few minutes to identify the right residence hall.

When I finally found his door and knocked, there was only silence. Of course there was. He was probably running a half marathon right now just to avoid me.

I knocked one more time, just to be sure. I thought I heard a rustle on the other side of the door.

Weird.

"Cax?" I called.

I heard a mumble. And then a groan.

"Are you alright?"

Again I heard a groan, and the hair stood up on my neck.

Was I even in front of the right door? Wondering if I was making a terrible mistake, I tried the knob, which turned willingly in my hand. "Cax?" I said, opening the door a few inches. "Are you okay?"

The studio apartment was even smaller than mine. The first thing I saw inside was a bed with tangled sheets. Cax's fully clothed body was lying on it. Then I noticed his hands were pressed into his eye sockets.

"Cax?" I forgot to worry about propriety and walked right in. The door closed behind me as I crossed the little room. I put a hand on his shoulder. "Are you okay?"

"Not really," he rasped. "Migraine."

I sat down on the bed. "Oh, I'm sorry. Do you get them often?"

"Only when I'm stressed out," he muttered. "So that's, like, pretty often."

"Poor baby." I dug my fingers into his shoulder muscle and squeezed. "You're so tight."

"That feels good."

"Turn over," I ordered him.

He flopped onto his stomach. I put both hands on his shoulders and began to rub. He moaned. "So good. Everything is in knots when my head aches."

I toed off my boots and climbed onto the bed, one knee on either side of his hips. I had better leverage up there. Massaging everything I could reach, I worked the stiff muscles in his shoulders. I kneaded his neck and rubbed the tight muscles at the back of his head. I worked my way up to his temples and went to town with the heels of my hands.

"You are the most amazing human," Cax mumbled. "Thank you."

"I could touch you all day, babe."

In some ways, he and I had the most confusing relationship in the world. We were close friends who didn't spend time together. We were lovers who rarely got even a kiss. We had a long history together with a big gap in the middle.

In short, we were a tangle of disasters. But there was nobody I'd ever felt so close to. Laying my hands on him felt like coming home. He felt like *mine*.

"Mmm," he sighed under my touch. "Wait. What time is it?"

"Almost three."

Cax groaned. "Damn. It. I have to go pick up Scotty from school."

My touch was light now, just fingertips on his forehead. "Can you drive like this?"

"I'll go slow," he said. "I don't have any peripheral vision, though."

"What?"

"It's called an ocular migraine—the edges of your vision go dark. It's creepy as hell but it always goes away."

That *did* sound creepy as hell. "Don't drive like that. I'll do it. I'll drive your car." I climbed off him.

Cax let out a sigh. "Would you? I'm not doing so well."

I could see that. "Come on. Where are your keys?"

"THE SCHOOL IS UP HERE on the right," Cax said. He covered his eyes with his hands.

"The glare is killing you, isn't it?" I asked. There was an inch or two of new snow on the ground. It made the town glisten. The sun had come out to sparkle on every white surface.

"Yeah. But tomorrow I'll be fine. Just have to keep telling myself that. It always goes away."

I pulled to a stop behind the line of cars at the curb. "The kids are starting to come out now."

Cax dragged his hands off his eyes and sat up straighter. He wore an uncomfortable squint that made me ache for him.

"Here." I took off my sunglasses and passed them to him. "Put these on."

He accepted them without argument. "Thanks for driving. Some high school kids have been giving Scotty trouble on the bus, and I've been picking him up on the days when I'm not teaching."

"Poor kid." I'd been there.

"My asshole father is no help. He told Scotty to punch somebody and then they'd leave him alone. As if a sixth-grader can clock a high school junior on a crowded bus and live to tell about it. Dad lives in a parallel universe where a real man can take down a bully by merely emitting a bit of testosterone into the atmosphere."

"Here he comes." I saw a skinny kid approaching the car, a smile on his face. When he got close enough to see his brother in the passenger's seat, his expression became curious.

"Hey," the boy said, opening the back door. "You okay?"

Jeez. Sharp kid. I hated wondering why he'd jump to the conclusion that something was wrong with Cax.

"I'm just having a migraine headache," he said. "I'll be fine tomorrow. But my friend Axel offered to drive, so I took him up on it."

"Hi Scott," I said.

"Hey, Axel. You work at the basketball games, right?"

"Sure do."

The kid pulled the car door closed. "You keep the stats?"

"Negative," I said. "Stats would be awesome, but I'm just handling the Twitter feed, and I write articles about the games for the alumni."

"No way! I liked that thing you did for the Yale game on Instagram. The bulldog rolling downhill?"

"Thanks!" I said, holding a hand back and over my shoulder, palm towards Scotty. He high-fived it. "Didn't know I'd meet a follower today."

Cax directed me to his father's house. Even his voice sounded pained.

"Did you take anything?" Scotty asked.

"Sure did, pal," Cax said, straightening up in his seat. "And when I get home, I'll take a hot shower. That always helps." He pointed up the block. "It's the brick... Oh, shit."

His father was on the front walk, shovel in hand. I recognized him after all this time—an older and grayer version of the sour man I remembered. He looked up just as I noticed him.

Tension radiated from Cax, so I stopped the car a distance away from where his dad stood. Cax clicked open the passenger-side door and got out just as Scotty did. Their dad walked towards us, an unreadable expression on his face. "Who's drivin' your car?" he asked.

"A friend from the department," Cax said, leaning on the open door. "Came down with a migraine at my desk today. It screws with my vision, so I asked for a hand."

"You pussy," his father snarled. "A fucking headache takes you down?" He bent at the waist and stared into the car.

I was not, by nature, a fearful person. But the look that

man gave me practically froze my blood. After ten seconds of giving me the icy-glare treatment, he straightened and gave Scotty a rough nudge toward the house. "Don't know why you don't just take the fucking bus, anyway. You're a pussy, too. Learning it from your brother."

Scotty's narrow shoulders hunched as he stomped toward the house.

"I told you I don't want your friends hanging around the boys," his father said. And he said it *right in front of me!* As if I must have a contagious disease if I was hanging out with Cax.

Unbelievable.

"There's nothing wrong with my friends," Cax snarled.

The two of them stared each other down, and I found myself holding my breath, wondering how the confrontation would end. "I'm going," Cax said eventually. The words were like two chips of ice.

"You do that." His father lowered the shovel to the sidewalk and turned his back on us.

Cax got into the car. The second his door slammed, I pulled away.

We were turning onto the main road before Cax spoke again. "He's not usually home at this hour."

"I'm sorry," I said quietly. "The distance you've been keeping between us seemed a little paranoid before. But it doesn't anymore."

"Yeah, it's..." Cax swallowed hard. "He's not easy to describe. I knew he'd treat you like..."

"The Ebola virus," I finished.

"Stop the car," Cax said quickly.

I pulled over immediately, and Cax opened the door. Then he bent over and vomited in the snow.

My heart contracted with sympathy. I looked around the car for tissues. Cax was a tidy person—he'd have something around for messes. I opened his glovebox and—bingo—napkins from a fast-food restaurant. "Here, Cax," I said, leaning toward his open door.

"I'm sorry," he muttered, taking the napkin.

"Does this happen a lot with your headaches?"

With a sigh, he slid back into his seat and shut the door. "I don't *usually* puke, but this isn't the first time. Closing my eyes while you drove..." He groaned. "I won't do that again."

"Let's get you home."

WHEN WE PULLED into the parking lot beside his building, he thanked me again for driving him.

"You're not getting rid of me so easily," I said.

"Axel..." he protested.

"He's not *here*," I said quietly. "I'm so sorry that happened, and your dad is the biggest asshole I've ever met. But right at this moment he can't see us."

Wordlessly he climbed from the car. And he didn't argue when I followed him inside the building.

"Now, how can I make you more comfortable?" I asked after he'd brushed his teeth. "Cup of tea?"

"Sure. I'm going to shower for a minute."

I put his kettle on and found a box of peppermint tea to fix for him.

He came out of the bathroom a couple of minutes later wearing only boxers. His hair was wet and his skin pink from the hot water. "I feel a little better now."

I put the mug in his hand. "Lie down. I'll rub your neck a little more before I go."

He took a sip, then put the mug on the nightstand. "I won't say no to that."

120

Straddling him once again, I let my hands play over all that bare, soft skin. "You are so beautiful to me," I whispered. "Kills me to see you feeling so ill."

He let out a long, shaky breath. "I'll sleep it off. That always works."

"Hope it will." I rubbed his neck, his head, his back. When my hands were too tired to continue, I lay down beside him. His face was turned away from me, but when I put a hand in the middle of his back, I felt him lean into my touch.

"Thank you," he whispered.

"Don't thank me," I returned, my voice hushed. "I meant to help you today, but I think I caused you trouble instead."

"Not your fault."

"I know, but..." I sighed. "There's no solution, is there?"

Rolling over to face me, Cax shook his head. "I've been trying to tell you that."

"I get it now." I moved closer, pulling him into my arms. He put his achy head on my shoulder. "I'm sorry."

"I know."

"I *pushed* you, though."

His arms pulled me even closer. "And I liked it."

Threading my fingers into his hair, I rubbed his scalp. "I love you, you know. Even if I'm not supposed to."

He was absolutely silent, so I feared that once again I'd gone too far. That was my specialty, apparently. I was about to apologize for the seventy-fifth time when Cax made a strange sound. And then another one. He was *crying*.

"Oh, hon. No!" I crooned, my palm holding his head against my chest. "I'm sorry. You need to sleep and—"

"It's just the pain, and..." He shook his head, his forehead rubbing against my shoulder. "No, actually. It's *not* just the headache talking. I *ache* for you. Every night I lie in this fucking bed and try to find a workaround..." He paused to swallow hard. "Never can."

Now my eyes were hot, too. "If there was anything I could ever do to help you, I'd do it."

He let out another shuddering breath. I could feel how hard he was trying to control himself. And my heart broke again with each unhappy noise he made.

"I should go," I whispered. Today I finally understood. Getting close to Cax only hurt him. That was just the way things were.

"Don't," he whispered. "Not just yet."

"Okay." I could never refuse him anything. Not when he was lying in my arms with tears on his face. I brushed them away with my thumb.

"I love you, too." He said it in an unhappy voice, though.

Ouch.

I squeezed him again to show that I understood.

Everything sucked. And not in a good way.

CHAPTER FIFTEEN

Caxton

I woke up the next morning with no headache. My relief lasted only until I sat down in my office and checked my email. There was a new message from Scotty.

Dad wanted to know who drove us home yesterday, so I told him your friend who worked at the basketball games. But after I said Axel's name, Dad got all super ragey. I went in my room and didn't come out until dinner, but he didn't ask me anything more. What is his damage?

"Oh, fuck," I whispered to myself. Axel was an unusual name. I should've realized that Scotty would repeat it and that my father might remember it from all those years ago.

My head gave a throb. Fanfuckingtastic. I got up and pulled on my coat, walking immediately to Starbucks for a cappuccino with a shot of caramel in it. I did not have time for more pain.

The one-two punch of caffeine and sugar seemed to work. So when I sat down at my desk, I looked up the number for Axel's office, and I called him.

"Hey!" he said after I greeted him. "I was just thinking about you. Are you doing better?"

"Yes and no," I said quietly. "My headache is gone, but my father is apparently on the warpath."

There was a silence on the other end of the line. "Shit. I'm sorry."

"I know you are." I was so sick of the two of us apologizing to each other when it was the rest of the world that caused us the real trouble. "But I've got to...cut off contact for a while."

"I understand," he said quickly. "Anything you need."

"It's not that I think he's reading my fucking email account, or anything. But I can't stay away from you. I'm going to get myself in trouble."

"I get it. I didn't before, but now I do. I..." He sighed into the phone. "If you ever need a hand, Cax, just call. Seriously. Even if it's a year from now and I haven't seen your face. You have a problem and I'm *there*."

My heart shimmied in my chest for two reasons. First, that I could go a year without him. And second, that he would say such a loving thing. "You kill me. You really do. I wish there was something I could do..."

"Just take care of yourself, would you? Do that for me."

The lump in my throat was basketball-sized. "You too."

"Goodbye for now," he whispered.

"Goodbye," I said, my voice breaking on the word.

I hung up the phone, my throat burning. Before Axel came to Henning, I'd only *suspected* that my life sucked. Now I knew that it truly did.

CHAPTER SIXTEEN

Axel

The next couple of weeks after Cax's phone call were rough.

I was lonely, and I missed emailing him. There were a few moments when I forgot to be lonely—when some funny thing on the Internet made me smile. And then I'd want to tell Cax about it.

Yep. Sad again.

So I put all my energy into my job. The team went on that trip to Providence, and we won. And I mostly succeeded in not thinking about Cax, who was undoubtedly at his brother's holiday concert like he said he would be.

Then the holidays happened. I bought a ticket to Ohio and moped around my mother's house for a few days.

"Will you tell me what's wrong?" she asked me one afternoon, running a hand through my hair as I sat at the kitchen table. "Aren't they good to you at work?"

I hadn't planned to tell her. She slid a mug of cocoa and a plate of Christmas cookies toward me, looking worried.

"They are perfectly good to me at work. But...do you remember Cax Williams?"

She blinked. "Who could forget him?"

The whole story came tumbling out. Except for the sexy bits. I definitely skimmed right over those.

When I was through she gave a dramatic sigh. "That poor boy. I want to punch his father right in the kisser."

"Aside from that, though," I grumbled. "I keep thinking about his situation, trying to find a workaround. There's no solution."

"He already told you his solution." My mother covered my hand with her own. "It's just that you don't like it."

I stared into the dregs of my cocoa. "I can't believe I found him again, but we still can't be together. And he wants to..."

"It's the pits," my mom agreed. "Tell me more about this Jason guy, though. At least he's available."

Why does it hurt so much when mothers are right?

AFTER MY WEEK OF VACATION, I went back to Henning determined to get out more and mope less. My poor little bank account wasn't quite so strained now that I'd had a couple of months of paycheck deposits.

Josh and Caleb invited me out for an evening at a place called Ralph's Tavern, and I accepted. It was a few miles out of town, though, so I'd planned to ride with them. But at work I got the idea to invite Boz to go with us. "You'll have to drive," I told him. "But I'll buy the first round."

"Ralph's is fun," he said. "But I got all excited there thinking you were asking me out on a date. When really I'm just your chauffeur. Way to crush my dreams." He threw a Barmuth teddy bear into the air and caught it.

"We'll find you a nice girl at Ralph's," I promised.

"But you'll be riding home again in my car." He grinned.

"How can I make all my smooth guy moves with you listening in?"

"If they were really that smooth, you wouldn't mind an audience."

"You are full of excuses." He looked at his watch. "When do we leave?"

Given Boz's allergy to working overtime, we left the office at 5:01 and beat Josh and Caleb to the tavern. We were already on our second beers when my neighbors arrived with a couple of Caleb's work buddies from the garage. "This is Danny and this is Jakobitz," Caleb said as we shook hands.

"Are you a couple, too?" Boz asked the other two mechanics.

Josh and Caleb burst out laughing.

"Are you KIDDING ME?" Danny yelled, pointing at Jakobitz. "He has the smelliest farts. If I was gay and he was the last man on earth..."

"Oh, as if *you're* so appealing," Jakobitz said with a disgusted look on his face. "Please. That mustache..."

"Whoops," Boz muttered.

"I'll bet you ten bucks that I'm the first guy to get hit on tonight," Danny said.

"Twenty says it's me," Jakobitz countered.

Caleb rolled his eyes.

My plan worked. I had fun in spite of myself. We ate pulled-pork sandwiches while Caleb and his friends told us a story about a customer who was convinced that a snake was lurking somewhere in his engine.

"He felt something slither across his ankle," Danny said. "But I think maybe the guy was just nuts."

"But can't a snake hide in an engine like that?" Josh asked. "I heard of that on Car Talk."

"In Texas, maybe," Caleb said, squeezing his husband's

shoulder. "How many snakes are slithering around in January in Massachusetts?"

"Good point. Did you look at his engine anyway? Maybe a snake escaped from a neighbor's house."

"We looked," Jakobitz said. "But only for a half hour, because we didn't want to charge this guy a fortune for a fool's errand."

"Could have been a mouse," Danny pointed out. "Mice make nests in cars all the time. But we didn't find any droppings."

Boz shuddered. "Now I have to worry about mice in my vehicle? Thanks for that."

"Set traps in your garage," Josh offered.

"Hi there! Excuse me?"

We all looked up to see a redheaded woman leaning into our conversation. She put a hand on Caleb's forearm. "It's my friend's birthday. Her." She tipped her head toward a table in back.

All our heads swiveled to look, of course. At the other table another girl sat alone, blushing profusely.

"Is there any way you could do a shot with us while I sing her Happy Birthday?"

"Uh," Caleb said, looking stunned by the offer. "My husband hates it when I get drunk."

She blinked.

"But there's six of us," Boz said quickly. "We can sing Happy Birthday really loudly. Trust me. Ready boys? What's your friend's name?"

"Suzie," she said, brightening up.

"On three! One, two, three..."

We all turned around and sang Happy Birthday to Suzie. And then Boz went over and bought her a shot and asked her if she wanted to play pool.

The dude did have some moves. Go figure.

The party moved over to the pool tables and everyone played. Josh was weirdly good at pool. Nobody could beat him. And neither Danny nor Jakobitz had to pay each other twenty bucks, because Caleb was the one who'd been hit on first.

"Hey Caleb," I said later, when it was getting late. "Can I ride home with you guys? Looks like Boz has other plans for tonight."

We all watched as Boz kissed the birthday girl on her neck, then said something that made her blush.

"Of course you can ride with us," Caleb said. "Let's go."

We grabbed our coats. "Does Josh really hate it when you get drunk? Or was that just some weird excuse?"

Caleb laughed. "Just talking out of my ass. Though once he had to pick me up here when I was wasted. He and I had had this horrible fight, and I drove here and let Danny and Jakobitz get me plowed."

"The dude can't hold his liquor *at all*," Danny agreed.

I tried to imagine Josh and Caleb fighting and...I couldn't picture it. Not at all. But maybe I needed to stop imagining that everyone else's lives were perfect.

"That's why that excuse popped out. Memories." He put a hand on Josh's shoulder and squeezed. "Women never hit on me. She caught me by surprise."

"They hit on you all the fucking time," Danny scoffed. "You just don't notice. Should we say g'night to Boz? I don't want to mess with his momentum."

We all glanced at him in the corner of the bar, where he was now liplocked with Suzie.

"Night, Boz," I called out cheekily.

He gave me the thumbs up without breaking the seal of their kiss.

At least somebody would go home optimistic.

129

"YOUR FRIENDS ARE AWESOME," Boz said on Monday. "The weekend was killer."

"They *are* awesome. But I think the whole experience agreed with you. Is that a hickey?" I left my chair for a closer look at his neck.

"It might be." Boz spun his chair, ruining my view. "Suzie didn't leave my apartment until Sunday. And I'm seeing her again next weekend."

Well. At least one of us was having sex. "Can I show you something I've been working on? It's not as much fun as Suzie. But it's pretty fun."

"Sure. I'm getting dizzy anyway." He stopped the chair.

At first, Boz didn't really understand my idea. But I knew it was solid, so I kept up my explanation. "On Family Night any kid fourteen or under who wears a basketball jersey or any kind of Barmuth spirit wear will get in free."

"Um," Boz said, scratching his chin. "But kids' tickets are only four bucks. And a movie ticket is eight. I don't think the price tag is keeping people away."

"You're right—it isn't. But that's not the point. There are local families who don't know how much they'd enjoy attending a live game, right? Plus, people love to think they're getting something for free. They'll get that four-buck ticket for free and then spend the money at the concession stand. Either way it will sound as if Barmuth was giving a gift to the Henning community. Meanwhile, adult tickets cost eight bucks, and we fill the place up. People will have a good time, and then they'll come back. I'm trying to create a positive feedback loop."

Boz laughed. "Listen to the marketing major throw the buzzwords around."

130

"Admit it. You like it."

"I do. I just wish I'd thought of it myself." He rotated his chair again as our boss approached. "Arnie! Listen to this idea that Axel has. It's genius."

Arnie's face was grim, and he didn't respond to Boz. "Axel, would you come with me, please? I need a word."

I knew something was wrong just by the tone of his voice. Following him into his office, I closed the door before taking a seat. And when he opened his mouth and told me the problem, I was flabbergasted.

"Axel, I've just been notified by our compliance office that they've received a complaint of sexual harassment against you."

For several seconds I just sat there replaying the words in my head. "What? From *who?*"

He folded his hands in his lap. "An employee of the college has made a complaint that you sexually harassed a graduate student."

Something about that statement sounded off. "A graduate student is accusing me of harassment?"

"Well..." He hesitated. "It's most unusual. The complainant isn't the graduate student. A third party has made the accusation."

Seriously? "Do I even know any graduate students? This makes no sense." My stomach lurched as I reached the only feasible conclusion. "*Oh.* Hang on. Is the person I've supposedly harassed named Henry Caxton Williams?"

Arnie nodded slowly.

I blew out an angry breath. "That's insane, but now I understand why this is happening. The complaint is completely baseless—Cax and I are friends from way back. We used to go to the same church diocese retreats starting in the third grade. His father doesn't like the fact that I'm gay. And a few days ago he figured out that I'd moved here to Henning. He wasn't happy."

Arnie was silent for a long minute. "Axel, you need a lawyer."

"Why?" I nearly gagged on the word. "I haven't done anything wrong. If Cax's dad is the guy who filed the complaint, Cax would never support it. No matter how much of an asshole his father was trying to be." *Shit*. That was true, right? I felt sick wondering what Cax might do to hang on to his lie. Tendrils of doubt began to curl around my heart.

Maybe I *did* need a lawyer.

My boss massaged his temples. "Kid, I think I get what you're saying. But this Williams guy has worked at the college for years. He understands that sexual harassment claims go into an employee's file, and he wants you to have this stain against you. Do yourself a favor and talk to a lawyer before you respond to this claim. Don't even tell your friend about it. Any communication you have with him right now could compromise you."

How depressing. Cax and I were already avoiding each other, anyway. "Okay," I heard myself say. "Where can I find a lawyer who understands this issue?"

Arnie studied me with watery blue eyes. "I'll help you. But please tell me you never badgered this kid."

I gave my head a violent shake. "Never. He and I are very close. And that's the problem. It's he and his father who barely speak to each other."

He sighed. "What a fucked-up world this is. Lemme talk to my friend at the law school and we'll find you someone who can help."

When I went back to my desk I picked up my notes for Family Night. My hands were shaking.

ARNIE WAS true to his word. Not forty-eight hours later, I sat down with a young lawyer who had agreed to help me at a reduced rate. And thank God. I didn't have much money. Mr. Williams probably knew that, too. He was trying to scare me away.

I was afraid it might actually work.

The first billable hour I spent with my lawyer was a really uncomfortable one. He asked me to start at the beginning. So I told him about our debacle at camp when we were teenagers. And how I'd run into Cax at the basketball game. (I skipped the part about seeing him on the video, because it wasn't relevant.)

I had to tell him about Merryline, of course. Until you've described your pathetic sex life to a perfect stranger, you haven't lived.

I finished up by describing the confrontation I'd witnessed between Cax and his dad in front of their house, and the bad vibe I got off him.

"And that's it," I said. "I know I didn't do anything wrong. But I don't know how to make this go away."

Trevor—my new lawyer—looked thoughtful. "Here's what we're going to do. You need to accuse Mr. Williams of harassing *you*."

I stared back at him. "You want me to...*what?*"

He leaned back in his chair. "Think about it. Your best defense is a good offense. He's done this because he wants a mark on your permanent record. So you need to leave one on his."

"Wait a second." Now my head was spinning. "I don't see how I can make his bogus claim go away by making one of my own."

"But I think you can. If you accuse him of harassing you, the college will be required to investigate, which he does *not* want. And it's not bogus. He *is* harassing you, Axel. You're having sex with his son, so he's trying to get you fired. That's what sexual harassment looks like."

"There was no actual, uh, penetrative sex with his son," I said quietly.

Trevor rolled his bright blue eyes. "That is a technicality. You went to a hotel with him. Do not defend yourself by saying it didn't happen. Defend yourself by saying that his father has *no right to complain*."

I took a deep breath, because my lawyer was suddenly making a whole lot of sense. "You would make an excellent gay man, Trevor."

He laughed. "I'll remember that if my wife ever leaves me. In the meantime, with your permission, I'm going to write out a complaint. As your lawyer, I'd really advise that you sign it. It's the best way of making sure he knows that you will not run out of town with your tail between your legs."

"That's what he wants."

"Exactly. Don't give it to him."

I was still worried. "What is he going to do to me if I file the complaint, though? What's his *next* move?"

My lawyer tapped his pencil on the desk. "The obvious response is to withdraw his complaint. Then you'll withdraw yours, because without his yours is baseless."

"I'm afraid he'll punish his son." *Hell.* I was already terrified of that.

"But what's the alternative? You can't just roll over. If you do nothing, you'll end up telling a room full of people the details of your trip to Merryline. And you've just told me that your friend needs to stay in the closet. The best way to protect him is to shake off his father. You can't put the genie back in the bottle. But you can shut him up."

I dropped my head into my hands. "I'm so afraid for Cax. I wish I'd never invited him to that hotel."

Trevor's face was full of empathy. "You weren't trying to get him in trouble. You were trying to keep him out of it."

"It doesn't matter, though. The path to hell..."

"...will be bulldozed by your lawyer," Trevor quipped. "Now give yourself a break from worrying. I have a complaint to write."

"Thank you," I said, standing up. "Seriously..."

He nodded. "Please don't communicate with anyone about this case except your boss and your immediate family. It's especially important not to discuss it with *either* of the Williams men."

"Okay," I promised.

"We'll work through this. Just give me time to get our counterclaim lined up."

"I will."

"And see what you can do about getting our team to beat Harvard next weekend."

I shook my head. "That might be asking too much."

He waved me off. "Fine. I'll call you tomorrow or the next day."

CHAPTER SEVENTEEN

Caxton

Three weeks without speaking to Axel. Every day felt hollow. Even if cutting off communication with him had been the safe thing to do, I was still upset about it.

And I looked for him everywhere. When I crossed the quad, my gaze landed on every guy who might be Axel. I looked for him in the grocery store and in line at the coffee shop.

I didn't *try* to look for him. It's just that I couldn't figure out how to stop.

Sitting through Scotty's holiday concert, I kept wondering what he was up to—whether he'd found a gay bar in Providence and whether he went home alone. It practically drove me nuts sitting there in the school auditorium, wishing I was miles away.

"Want to go out for ice cream?" I asked Scotty when the concert was over.

"Isn't it kinda late?" he asked. That was Scotty, always clinging to the rules, hoping to stay out of trouble. Just like me.

How depressing.

"Just a quick cone," I said, hurrying him to the car. "I need something to celebrate."

"Okay," he said, humoring me. "Let's do it."

The holidays dragged by. The graduate housing complex emptied out. Sometimes my lonely reading light seemed like the only sign of life. I did some research for my dissertation, but often found my mind wandering.

I thought it would get easier when all the students came back after New Year's. Classes began on Monday, but, as I sat at a conference table with a new group of undergraduates, my sense of loneliness didn't disappear. They looked about a hundred years younger than I felt.

Beginning-of-semester things got posted in the teaching assistants' office. I did a quick scan of the intramural basketball schedule, hoping to see a game with the Athletic Department coming up soon. I found it, but it wouldn't happen for another month.

Sigh.

I spent long hours in the library. On Tuesday night, I realized I'd been staring into space for a long time. Calling it quits, I closed the tabs on my Internet browser. On a whim, I checked my work email one more time. There was a message from the compliance department.

That was odd.

DEAR MR. WILLIAMS,

Your presence is requested next Monday at 9:00 AM in Trainor Hall for a hearing regarding charges of sexual harassment. Please reference the complaint Henry Williams Sr. v. Axel Armitage.

I READ that message a dozen times, because it made no sense.

Then I thought about my father, and realized that it did.

I stood up so fast that my library chair went toppling backwards. Grabbing my coat, I marched out of the library, hurrying through the atrium. When I left the building, I did not go home. I did not go to my father's house, because that would leave me screaming at him in front of the boys. And I did not go to a bar to drink myself silly, although that wasn't a horrible idea.

Instead, I walked straight into College Park and onto the path to Axel's apartment.

He must be freaking out.

God *damn* it! He'd come here for a job. And he'd shown me nothing but love. And now my fucking father was going to drag him down into the muck. Axel. The man I loved. My heart *burned* for him.

I was really fired-up by the time I made it to the end of the wooded path, reaching the stairs up to his door. When I got to the top, my knock was too urgent. And when the door swept open, I stepped inside without waiting for an invitation.

"Cax," he said, backing up as I barged forward. "You shouldn't be here. There's trouble and—"

"Fuck the trouble!" I shouted. "He's the fucking devil. I can't take it anymore." I stood there, chest heaving, face red from the cold and from anger.

Axel looked so uncertain, and my heart broke at the sight of his uneasy eyes. "Babe, I'm not supposed to talk..."

"Then let's not *talk*." I closed the distance between us and put my hands on his chest. But the uneasy look in his eyes did not go away. So I grabbed his shirt in two hands and kissed him.

"Ummnf," he said, surprised. I wrapped a hand behind his neck and nipped his lower lip. I pulled him closer to me. I just had to. Enough with letting other people rule my life. For *years*

139

I'd tried to conform to my father's stupid rules, and it was nothing but a disaster.

Enough.

"Axel," I demanded, my lips against his mouth. "Kiss me."

He sighed, and my heart froze with fear. Was it already too late? Who would want a guy who had as much baggage as I did?

But then Axel's mouth softened under mine. His hands gripped my waist, and he kissed me gently. Another sigh slipped from his chest, and he gave in.

I was still too revved up by a thousand raw emotions to be gentle. I forced my tongue into his mouth, laving it against his. He groaned in reply, deepening the kiss. And then we were on the move. Axel nudged me toward the bed. I went, trying not to stumble over my feet. Between kisses, he nudged me again, and it wasn't gentle. Eager hands pushed me until my ass hit the bed. My coat was yanked roughly from my shoulders and thrown on the floor.

Now we were on exactly the same page. His kisses were just as urgent as mine, probably because he understood. It was now or never for us. The future was getting uglier by the minute. His job was in peril. My life was teetering on a cliff.

Here in Axel's apartment, there was only the present moment. And Axel was making quick work of the buttons on my shirt.

I kicked off my shoes. Then I grabbed the waistband of his pants and popped the button. I'd never done this before—just reached out to take what I wanted. It felt so fucking freeing to go where my heart led me. And when I unzipped him and then slipped my hand into his fly, there was a nice, thick cock waiting for me. I gave it a firm stroke and he hardened in my hand.

"Fuck," Axel choked out. The sound of his arousal lit me

up. Too much time had been wasted waiting for life to get better. I yanked his trousers down his hips, and they fell away like I needed them to. After he kicked them away, he grabbed his shirt, tugging it over his head. The hot, determined look on his face was everything I'd ever wanted.

After shedding my shirt, I shucked my jeans and underwear, then kicked off my socks. I was completely naked on Axel's bed. He stood above me, a hungry look on his face. "Come here," I ordered. I lay back and parted my legs. It felt like the dirtiest thing I'd ever done, but it was exactly what I needed right now. I needed him to fuck me.

And I needed to never, ever think.

Axel climbed onto the bed on his hands and knees. He was still wearing his briefs, so I reached up and tugged the waistband away from his beautiful skin. I plunged my hand inside and curved my hand around his cock.

He hissed, and the sound was beautiful to me. Then he shed his briefs and maneuvered his body the other way on the bed, so he was facing my toes. He dropped his face down to my groin and took the head of my dick in his mouth.

I gave a full body shudder. God, it felt so good. I reached between his legs, sifting my fingers through the soft hair of his inner thighs before cupping his balls in my hand.

He hissed again and I felt myself get even harder in his mouth. My hips twitched with yearning, and I was mad with want. I wanted to suck and fuck and rub off on him all at once. He dropped his head between my legs and I let out a bellow that could probably be heard for miles. Axel was sucking my balls, one at a time. "Turn over," he rasped.

Without hesitation I rolled onto my stomach. Axel moved, reorienting himself on the bed. Warm fingers tried to spread me. Then he grasped my hips and tugged. "On your knees."

I lifted my ass, and then his mouth was back, teasing my

taint with his tongue. "Oh Jesus," I gasped as a warm, wet tongue probed me. "Fuck me," I begged. "Please."

He placed a soft kiss on my inner thigh. "I plan to." He gave my ass a slap. "Spread for me."

I did. He disappeared for a moment, leaving me there, ass in the air, completely vulnerable.

And I loved it. This was exactly where I'd always needed to go. *Finally*.

A moment later I heard the sound of a lube bottle opening. Then Axel's hard body was behind me, his slicked-up fingers rubbing into my crease.

I took a deep breath and focused on relaxing. When he eased a finger inside me, I was ready. I pushed back against him, reaching for it. "More," I demanded.

Axel leaned down to kiss my back. "Got to take it slow," he murmured.

"Fuck slow. Been waiting too long for this."

I received another kiss on my spine. "Let me work you open. Then I'll give you the pounding you deserve."

Groaning, I dropped my elbows onto the bed. I felt a second finger press in to meet the first. There was a burn, but it was a burn that I wanted. "Yeah," I panted. My hips rocked back onto his hand. I was woozy with adrenaline and desire. He played with me while I panted, waiting.

My whole life I'd craved this—Axel's hands on my body. Axel owning me. All the anger I'd brought here with me today had morphed into desire. I was vibrating with need and desperation, pressing into him, fucking myself on his hand. "Please," I sobbed.

"Soon," he whispered.

All I could do was drop my face into the bedspread and moan. Fuck *soon*. I was done with *soon*.

Finally, I heard the crinkle of a condom wrapper and the

snap of the lube bottle again. "Ready, baby?" I felt the press of a nice hard dick against my hole.

With a deep groan I pushed back against him. For one awful moment I thought it wasn't going to work. And then my muscles relented and let him in.

Axel moaned as he sank inside. I was suddenly so *full* of him. I needed to close my eyes to adjust to the sensation.

Behind me, Axel took a slow breath and let it out. "You okay?" he asked.

I nodded because I was. But I was also overwhelmed. I'd been waiting years for this. My eyes were damp from the flood of emotion. Axel. Finally. *Yes...*

He rocked gently. "I'm going to move. You tell me if I hurt you, or if you find something you like."

Again, I nodded. Axel withdrew a little ways then pushed back inside. It was such a foreign sensation that I found myself holding my breath.

He ran a hand down my flank, gentle fingers almost tickling my ribs. "Breathe, honey. Relax for me. I need you loose. You are so fucking sexy." He pulled his hips back and then pushed forward all at once. "Mmm. Love fucking you."

The dirty talk was just what I needed. I spread my legs a little farther apart, opening myself to him. "Take me," I begged.

"I've got you. You're all mine now. Actually, turn over." He pulled all the way out.

"What? Why?"

He slapped my ass. "On your back. I need to see your face while I fuck you."

I flipped over, and then Axel lifted first one of my legs and then the other onto his shoulders. It was a strange position, yet I really loved the view—Axel smiling down on me. "Do it," I gasped.

His eyelids went half-mast as he pushed inside. "Oh, fuck. So good. So tight."

I adjusted my hips and took in the beautiful sight above me. Axel's sixpack tensed as he slowly fucked me. He breathed deeply through several thrusts. Then he began to move faster.

That's when it started. He shifted his stance a little bit, and my limbs began to tingle and burn. "Ahh..." I moaned.

"You like that?" He snapped his hips, canting them upward. Someone shouted, and it was me.

"That's right," he panted. "I'm going to pound that spot, and you're going to come so hard."

I was moaning now. Each thrust made me feel lightheaded. Something was building, and it wasn't like anything I'd felt before. I reached one shaking hand up to Axel's face, and he kissed it. Then he picked up the pace. "Love fucking you, baby. Touch yourself for me."

He moved my shaky hand onto my dick, encouraging me to stroke, but I was so busy being overtaken by the peculiar, whole-body arousal that I didn't put much effort into it.

Above me, Axel chuckled. Knocking my hand away, he began stroking my cock while he thrust. "I'm close, Caxy." He tightened his jaw, and I saw the strain in his neck as he tried to hold himself together.

He was so beautiful. And at least for this moment, he was all mine. My balls began to tighten, and I floated on the beauty of it all.

"Come for me, baby," he gritted out. With a grunt he gave me another big thrust, and I felt my arousal spill over in a wave of naked pleasure. I pushed my useless body against the bed and gasped. "Fuck, yeah," he panted. "Oh, fuck. Cax..."

In the distance I heard him grunting through his climax. But I was somewhere else. Everything went dim for a few moments.

When I came back into my body, Axel was kissing my jaw. "Baby," he whispered. "You okay?"

"Yessss," I sighed. "That was..." Trying to describe it wasn't going to get me anywhere. "So crazy. Outrageous."

"Did you like it?"

"Hell yes." There was only a small pool of jizz on my stomach. "Weird—I didn't come very much."

He kissed my shoulder. "Prostate orgasms are a whole different species. Some people don't even stay hard when they come."

"I don't think I can move my limbs," I whispered.

"Then don't."

I closed my eyes. Axel moved about the room, but I wasn't concerned with why. A minute later a warm, damp cloth was used to wipe off my belly. And a while after that, gentle hands eased the covers down, encouraging me to move just enough to get underneath. I made room for Axel in his own bed.

"Mmm," I said when warm arms curled me close to him.

"That was perfect," he breathed in my ear.

"Yes," I agreed, almost too tired to speak. "Thought it would never happen. Thought it was over."

"With the way I feel about you? It's never over," he said with a sigh.

"Love you," I ground out. Then I let him hold me while I fell all the way to sleep.

CHAPTER EIGHTEEN

Axel

I woke up tangled in Cax. It was so nice to have him in my bed that when my alarm went off, I chose not to move after shutting it off. I was going to be late to work today.

Fuck it.

After a while, Cax turned away from me, burying his face in the pillow. He was probably too warm, but I didn't want to stop touching him. So I traced his smooth back with my fingertips, and when I reached his waist, he shivered.

This was really all that I'd ever wanted. Cax in my bed, naked.

I placed my lips on his neck and kissed him. Nibbled him. Sucked on his skin. And all the while I let my hand drift lazily down his body and then over his hip. He groaned when I found a hard dick pointing straight up against his belly. I started stroking him slowly, but he rolled to face me.

"Good morning," I whispered.

"Oh, yes it is," he returned. Then he leaned in to kiss me.

So much for slow and lazy. A few seconds later we were making out like frantic people. He rolled on top of me, his hips riding mine. His tongue was so deep in my mouth that I didn't know where he ended and I began.

I grabbed his ass and squeezed. Cax moaned loudly. "Ax, unless you tell me not to, I am going to come incredibly soon."

"Do it," I encouraged.

But he rose up on all fours instead, and a second later, he slid my cock into his mouth. "Fuck, baby," I moaned. My hips rolled, because I could not stay still. He tongued me, his kisses wet and sloppy. *Heaven.* And then he opened wide and gave me one good, hard suck. "Oh, damn. I'm close."

Releasing me, Cax moved up the bed to lay beside me. I rolled to face him, taking his mouth in a deep kiss. Our hands tangled as we each grabbed the other's cocks, Cax's fingers beginning to slide up and down my shaft. I pumped into his hand, and he did the same into mine. I gave him one more kiss and then pulled back to watch his face.

His eyes were dark and heavy with lust. "Love you," he mouthed. Then his lips parted on a moan, and he began to shoot in my hand. I followed him a second later, coming all over us while staring into his eyes.

We were left panting and sated—a sticky pile of limbs and damp skin and kiss-swollen mouths. I levered myself up on an elbow, then leaned down to give him a single, soft kiss on the lips. Then I collapsed again.

It was several minutes before either of us spoke. "We need a shower," I said finally.

"You need a lawyer," was Cax's reply.

I stroked his nipple with my thumb. "Already got one," I said quietly.

He sighed. "I'm so sorry."

"It's not your fault."

"I'll tell the truth," he said. "I'll go into that hearing and tell everyone that I love you, and that my father can't handle it."

"You might not have to do that. I'm not supposed to talk to you about this, but yesterday I signed—"

"Don't tell me if you shouldn't," he said quickly. "But know this—I will tell the truth, even if it makes my life more difficult than it already is."

My chest felt tight just thinking about that. "I don't want you to get cut off from your brothers."

"I *know* that. But I might, and it won't be your fault. I'm *gay*, Axel. And my father has always known it. For years I've been avoiding this showdown, but it was always coming for me. I'm almost relieved."

I snorted. "What you are is sexually satisfied. For the first time ever."

Cax poked me in the ribs. "And you're *smug*."

"And sticky. Come on." I tugged his hand. "Time for the clean-up."

WE WERE GETTING DRESSED when there was a knock on the door. I checked Cax's face and saw panic there.

"Hey, it's okay," I whispered.

His expression went sheepish. "I've been afraid my whole life. That's not going to turn around on a dime."

"I know." I liked the way he put that, though. As if he was looking forward to a different future. "Why don't you step into the bathroom until I see who it is?"

He slipped past me and I went to the door. Whoever it was knocked again just as I turned the knob. "Axel?"

I opened the door to Josh. "Hey. Morning. Something wrong?"

He frowned. "I'm not sure. I just found the weirdest letter in yesterday's mail. Someone must have stuck it into our mailbox—without postage. I haven't showed it to Caleb yet. But the whole thing looks scammy." He offered me a piece of paper that had been folded into thirds.

It was printed on Barmuth College stationery. *"To whom it may concern: Mr. Axel Armitage has been accused of sexual harassment by his employer. Should the accusation result in his termination, his landlord should be aware that he will no longer have sufficient funds to afford his lodgings. Sincerely, the Human Resources Department."*

I sighed. "Motherfucker."

"What did he do now?" Cax came out of the bathroom, blowing his own cover.

Josh's eyes got wide before he recovered, hiding his surprise. "Good morning, Mr. Williams."

"You don't have to call me Mr. Williams anymore. You're no longer in my section." Cax crossed the room and read the letter over my shoulder. "That is just ridiculous. I'm going to kill him."

Josh crossed his arms. "Can I ask who?"

"My father," Cax grumbled. "He's trying to railroad Axel. This isn't the worst of it, either."

Josh's face softened. "I'm sorry. Is it because you two...?" He left the question unfinished.

"Absolutely," I said. "But I've hired a lawyer, and I'm trying to get him to back off. As of right now, there's no reason to assume I won't make the rent."

"I'm not worried," Josh said quickly. "I understand what you're going through. Where Caleb and I come from, they would have come after us with a shotgun. Just let us know if we can help in any way."

"Thank you," I said. "Really—I appreciate that."

Josh smiled. "Come for dinner tomorrow night. Both of you."

"Okay," Cax said quickly, surprising me. I raised my eyebrows at him. "I want to," he said quietly. "I'm done trying to please him."

"But..." I was worried for Cax. "We still don't know what's going to happen. Your brothers..."

"I know," he said, putting a hand on my arm. "But I just can't do it anymore. I tried to manage the situation, and I failed. He wants a confrontation. I can't stop him. And I'm sick of walking away from you. That's *cowering*, Axel. I'm so done with the whole thing."

"Okay," I said softly. I looked up at Josh, who had been listening quietly. "Two for dinner. I'll bring something. Just tell me what—a side dish? A salad?"

"A salad," he said. "We'd never eat one otherwise."

"Fine." I laughed.

"Seven o'clock," he said.

"Awesome," Cax replied. "We'll be there. And I'll bring wine. I'll probably need some."

"Deal."

WITH JOSH'S PERMISSION, I kept the weird letter in order to show it to my lawyer.

"I'll leave now, because you're already late for work," Cax said, stepping into his shoes.

I caught up to him before he got to the door. "Hey. Kiss me," I whispered. He did, and it was so fucking sweet. I ran my hand gently over his ass. "Are you sore?"

Cax blushed. "A little. But I don't mind."

I kissed him one more time, but then I had to release him

or I'd never make it to work. "Are you feeling all right? Would you tell me if you weren't?"

"Mostly, and yes," he said, grabbing his coat. "I don't want my life to fall apart. But if it's inevitable, I'll deal, okay? Let's just see what happens. And if he gets uglier with us, we'll console ourselves with more sex."

I laughed. "All right." I liked this new, tougher Cax. I liked him a lot. But I was still uneasy. There was something about his father's weird letter to Josh and Caleb that smacked of desperation. "You should probably stay out of your father's way until next week. That's when—"

"The hearing. I know." He buttoned his coat. "I'll make myself scarce."

"Tell me if you hear anything weird from him," I begged.

"I will." He stepped forward and gave me a quick kiss. "I'll see you tomorrow night at seven." Then he left.

Thirty minutes later I ran into work, late. I sat down in my chair and tried to gather my thoughts. I needed to call my lawyer about the letter and to confess that Cax and I had been friendlier than I'd planned.

"Somebody got laid!" Boz hissed. "Damn. *Finally*. Tell me who it was so I can thank him personally. I was getting tired of the long face."

I looked up in surprise. "Don't know what you're talking about."

"Dude, you're sitting there just smiling at your computer's login screen. And you're an hour later than usual. You might as well paint it on your forehead."

Good grief. "What was your major at Barmuth, anyway?"

"Psychology," he said with a chuckle. "And just admit it. I'm pretty brilliant."

"You're pretty annoying is what you are." Ignoring his laugh, I finally got down to work.

Later, when I called the lawyer, he said he wanted to see the letter that Josh had received. So at lunchtime I ran it over to his office.

"This is weird," he said, squinting at the text. "It's so clumsy."

"That's what I thought, too."

He slipped it into a plastic sleeve. "You never know—we might end up dusting it for fingerprints."

"He's ex-military," I pointed out. "He teaches a course on the history of U.S. Intelligence. He probably wore gloves."

Trevor shook his head. "I don't get this guy. If he's so tactical, why is he running around like a nut delivering letters? Be careful, okay? If you see him anywhere, just get the hell away."

I didn't like the sound of that. "Okay. There's something else I have to tell you, too."

"Why am I suddenly worried?"

"Well, I tried to stay away from Cax, but it didn't work out like I'd planned." I explained how Cax had practically broken down my door last night after learning about the sexual harassment claim, and I confessed that he'd spent the night.

Trevor didn't admonish me. Instead, he looked thoughtful. "It's clear that Cax is feeling a lot of pressure right now. It won't be easy for him if he's asked to choose between the people he loves."

"He's in a tough place," I admitted. *Ugh.* I wasn't looking forward to the look on Cax's face if his father tried to cut him off from his brothers. "But he won't incriminate me to make his father happy. He just wouldn't do that. If the college asks him if I harassed him, he's going to say no." Whether our poor, doomed relationship would survive it, I had no idea. But Cax wouldn't throw me under the bus to keep his family together. Of that I felt certain.

Trevor nodded. "Okay. I'll let you know if I hear anything

back about the complaint we made. I'm expecting to hear something very soon. They have to respond."

"Thank you," I said.

"Hang in there."

I SPENT the rest of the afternoon designing a newspaper advertisement for Family Night. And then I tried to figure out what silly pictures a guy could tweet out when his team was playing Harvard. The oldest (and snootiest) college in the country didn't have a cute, furry mascot. The big red H wasn't easy for me to mock, damn it.

Around three o'clock I got an email that I enjoyed.

Caxtastrophe to Axeldental: *You know those modern kiosks at the library? I'm standing at one of them, grading essays. Sitting down isn't all that comfortable today. (Totally worth it.)*

Axeldental to Caxtastrophe: *Hope you're okay. Because last night changed my life for the better.*

Caxtastrophe to Axeldental: *I need to be as good as new by tomorrow. Because I want a repeat.*

Axeldental to Caxtastrophe: *If you're still sore, we'll just have to switch things up.*

Caxtastrophe to Axeldental: *Huh. Oh—the pain! It's gotten worse all of a sudden.*

Axeldental to Caxtastrophe: *Maybe I could kiss it better.*

Caxtastrophe to Axeldental: *And now I'm hard in the library, standing at a kiosk. Walk on by, folks. Nothing to see here. *Ducks behind a Greek statue**

Axeldental to Caxtastrophe: *Can't wait to see you for dinner tomorrow. Actually, let's talk tonight? Can I call you around ten? I want to say goodnight. And a few other things. Pajamas optional.*

Caxtastrophe to Axeldental: *Great. I'm free then. But now I'm stuck behind a statue for the foreseeable future. And I think I hear a tour coming. I'm just going to stare at this statue. But it's a nude of course, and his ass reminds me of yours. Maybe my father is right. I'm a hopeless perv. I'm perving on a marble statue.*

Axeldental to Caxtastrophe: *You're a perv, but you're my perv.*

By the time I left the office, it was dark, and I couldn't stop thinking about phone sex. I was a phone sex virgin, because I'd never been with someone who wanted me badly enough to try it. But I supposed I could figure it out.

There was only a smattering of new snow on the ground, so I headed through the park via the wooded path. If I survived Mr. Williams's attack on my career, and lived over Josh and Caleb's garage for years, I might need to invest in a pair of snowshoes. That might be fun.

I wasn't the only person in the park. A female jogger passed me, running in the opposite direction. Massachusetts was a sportier place than Ohio. Henning was the sort of town where people jogged through the park in thirty-degree weather with mittens on.

The sky was purple-black, though I could see a glow rising behind the Berkshires. There would be a moon tonight, but it hadn't yet poked its head above the hilltops. I whistled as I continued my trek. At some point I thought I heard footsteps behind me, but I didn't turn around.

But I should have.

When the attack came, I was so close to home I could see the shimmer of porch lights on Newbury Street. One moment I was walking, then the next something collided forcefully with my head. I hit the ground, sprawling on the path, tasting dirt and snow. My head felt like it had been split in two, and I couldn't think why.

Reflexes demanded that I try to stand up. But I didn't get past an elbow on the ground before a kick landed at my ribs.

I shrieked at the pain.

"Shut it, cocksucker." My assailant had a voice full of gravel.

I knew that voice. But there was no time to think about it. I writhed away from the sound of him, curling in on myself. Once again, I tried to roll to a vertical position. But a knee came out and connected with my temple.

"Think you can threaten me?" the voice said from somewhere in the wavering distance. "Stupid faggot. Get the fuck away from my son."

A foot connected with my eye socket, and there was more blinding pain.

The last thing I remembered was my head bouncing off the hardpack.

Then nothing.

THE NEXT TIME I came to consciousness, I was burning hot. Especially one side of my face.

Weird.

My phone was ringing, too. I knew it was my phone, because the ring tone was "We Will Rock You" by Queen. But I really just wanted the noise to stop.

"Oh my God," somebody said. Someone familiar. "Oh my God. Axel?"

Hands landed on me, and I flinched. Everything hurt.

"Oh, no. Oh my God." The voice belonged to Josh.

We will ROCK YOU!

Josh made the phone's noise stop. "Hello?" he said, his voice anxious. "Who's this? Boz! Axel is hurt. Someone…

Someone hurt him, I think. We're outside... You know where College Park is? There's a path into the woods behind the swing sets. What? Okay—you're right. I'm calling them right now."

Then he was speaking to me again. "Axel, I have to call 911. Hang with me."

I thought I saw a flash of blue light, probably made by my phone. For a moment, the only sound was Josh's heavy breathing. He sounded panicked, but I wasn't quite sure why. "Yes, this is an emergency," I heard him say.

After that, I stopped listening. There was only blackness.

CHAPTER NINETEEN

Caxton

I was lying in my bed at ten o'clock sharp, wearing only boxers. Hadn't Axel said he'd call me? Was I supposed to call him?

It was dawning on me that for the first time in my adult life, I might get the chance to be in a real relationship. And that I had no earthly idea how to be in one.

Call? Or wait?

I'd give it five more minutes. Lying on my bed, I tried to think about the Bull's season. But really, I could only think of Axel. Sex with Axel...

My phone rang and I snatched it up happily. "Hello? Axel?"

"Cax? It's Gil. Who's Axel?"

It took me a second to get over my disappointment, which was ridiculous. Gil, my college roommate, was one of my favorite people. And I hadn't talked to him in quite a while. "Hey! Sorry. I totally owe you a call."

He chuckled. "Yeah, you totally do. How's the grad-student thing going?"

"Pretty good," I said. But that was just the easy answer, and maybe I needed to stop ducking questions from all the people in my life who were good to me. "Actually, it's been a tricky year so far. Plenty of good stuff, but some trouble, too."

"With school?" he asked.

"Nope. Actually, there's something I've been needing to tell you for a while."

"Is that so?" There was a hint of amusement in his voice, and I didn't understand why.

But I forged ahead. "Yeah, well. All those times you told me to break up with Amy so I didn't sit home every weekend?"

"Don't tell me you *did* it?"

I chuckled. "I couldn't really break up with her, because we weren't really a thing. I'm gay, Gil. I just never wanted to tell you. Or anyone."

He snorted. "I know that, moron. Glad you finally decided to admit it."

"You...what?" Something swerved inside my chest, and not in a good way. I didn't care what Gil knew about me, but I didn't like to hear that I couldn't fool people when I needed to.

"Dude. Nobody waits around for their girlfriend for four years like that. Well, maybe some guys do. But at least they fuck her senseless when she comes to visit. I always knew you guys were just friends. I never saw you look at her like maybe you wanted to eat her for dinner."

I sighed. "Fair enough."

"I'll just stop right there," he said with a chuckle.

"Why? There were other signs?"

"Maybe," he said, and I could hear his smile through the phone. "The cross country team used to run down our block shirtless, in those spandex shorts."

I snorted. "I remember."

"Is Axel a long-distance runner? Because I think you have a thing for cross country."

160

"God, Gil. I can't believe we're having this conversation." It was trippy to tell the truth.

"Well, are you?"

"He's a basketball player," I said.

"Close enough!" We both laughed. "I'm sorry to let the air out of your tires, Cax. But it's a relief to hear you telling the truth. And finding what you're looking for."

I didn't know how to reply to that. Gil cared enough about me to say these things, and it made me feel like a shitty friend. "Regardless, it's good to talk to you. How's the new job?"

"Boring. I think I'm going to apply for law school. I hate Wall Street."

"Ouch."

"Yeah. Don't feel too bad for me, though. The money is good. And I save it all, since I'm working too many hours to spend it. I'm at work right now."

"At ten fifteen?" It was getting late. I wondered what had happened to Axel.

"Yeah. I'm about ready to head home. I just wanted to say hi before another week went by."

"I'm really glad you did," I said. "It's been too long."

"We'll talk soon, okay? You can tell me more about this basketball player."

"All right. But I have to ask you not to say anything to anyone we know. My father…"

"Still the world's biggest asshole?"

"Yeah."

"I'm a vault, Cax. Thanks for telling me, finally. And congratulations."

We hung up a moment later, and I squinted at my phone, just in case Axel had tried to reach me and I'd missed it. While I was doing that, someone knocked on my door.

I smiled. It wasn't a great idea for Axel to come to my

place, but if he had, I'd be really excited to see him. I hopped out of bed.

Then again, if it wasn't Axel, I was really underdressed right now. "Who is it?" I asked, yanking my robe off the hook on the bathroom door.

"It's the Henning police. Please open the door immediately."

My throat went dry. I did as the man said, opening the door to two uniformed officers. "Can I help you?"

"Are you Henry Caxton Williams, Junior?"

I nodded.

"When is the last time you saw Axel Armitage?"

Oh no. I grabbed the door frame for support. "Why?"

"Please answer the question. Have you seen him tonight?"

I shook my head. "This...this morning. When I left his apartment."

The officer seemed to stare me down. He had a mustache, and for some reason I decided that was a good sign. He was too comical-looking to be handing me awful news. "What's your relationship with Mr. Armitage?"

"He's..." I'd never said this out loud. "He's my boyfriend."

The mustached officer nodded. "We need you to come to the station with us and answer a few questions."

"Why? What's this about?"

"Axel Armitage is unconscious in a hospital bed tonight. We want to know why."

The room did a dip and a roll.

"He's going down," the other officer said.

But I hung on to the doorjamb and braced my knees. "Tell me what happened."

Mustache Man frowned. "You have to come with us. We'll sort this out."

"No way." I had to go to the hospital. Except I couldn't

162

think straight. Where were my keys? And my mind was stuck on the word *unconscious*. And the warmth in Axel's eyes as he kissed me goodbye this morning. I turned around on shaky legs to find some jeans and a sweatshirt.

"You come with us right now or we'll have to bring you in."

I ignored him, looking for my shoes.

The cop sighed. "Fine. We'll do this the hard way. You have the right to remain silent. Anything you say can be used against you in a court of law…"

"Wait, what?" This guy was reading me my Miranda rights. "What are you doing?"

"You have the right to an attorney. If you cannot afford one…"

This could not be happening.

CHAPTER TWENTY

Axel

Ow. My head was killing me. And I couldn't seem to open my eyes. There was something covering them.

Weird.

I was in bed. But it wasn't my bed. There were low voices nearby. I knew one of the voices, but I usually heard it at work. "Boz?" I tried to say my coworker's name, but my throat was so dry that it came out as a scrape.

The talking ceased. "Axel? Did you say something?"

"Where am I? What's this?" I tried to raise a hand to touch the thing on my eyes. But only one of my hands moved, and it was as heavy as an anvil.

"Oh," another male voice said. "Careful."

"Um, Josh?" I was pretty sure I heard my landlord now. This was one hell of a weird dream I was having.

My hand was clasped between two big, warm hands. I knew it was Josh from the sound of the sniffle he emitted. "It's good to hear your voice," he said.

That confused me. "Why?"

He cleared his throat. "You've been out for more than twelve hours. We were starting to panic."

I tried to understand why that might be. But I couldn't quite grasp it.

So I slept.

THE NEXT TIME I woke up I heard my mother's voice. Now *that* was weird. "Mom?"

There was a sharp intake of breath. "Axy? Oh, sweetie. Please wake up."

"Why?"

Her laughter sounded a little manic. "Because I'm worried sick about you. Keep talking."

"Thirsty."

She made a little throaty gasp, which I recognized as her fighting off tears. "Let me call the nurse."

They brought me a drink of water, which I sipped through a straw. "My jaw is killing me," I complained.

"You took several kicks to the head," my mother said, her voice grave. "You don't know how happy I am to hear you speaking to me right now."

"Why can't I open my eyes?"

She sniffled again. "You had eye surgery for a detached retina."

"Gross."

There was a muffled sob. "It could have been so much worse," she said, her voice breaking.

The longer this conversation went on, the more aware I became of my injuries. "He got my ribs," I said.

"I'm sorry, baby."

One of my arms was pinned to my body, too. "What else?" I asked. "Tell me the worst."

"Your arm is broken. But it's not too bad. And they're

watching some internal bleeding. To make sure you don't need another surgery. So far, so good."

"What about my face?"

She let out a shuddering breath. "You are really bruised. Quite like a horror movie, actually. But there's only one bad cut, on your cheekbone. You can decide later if you want plastic surgery for the scar."

That didn't sound too bad. Any time a doctor said "decide later" that meant it wasn't dire. "And my eye?" That was by far the creepiest thing she'd said.

"The doctor will come by later," she whispered. "They'll take off the bandage and check your vision."

I felt a little shimmy of fear at the sound of that. My vision was pretty damned crucial. There was one question I still had to ask. "Where's Cax?"

She sighed. "He has some things to deal with."

"But he's okay?"

"He's fine, honey. Nobody hurt Cax."

"Where's his dad? He's the one who..."

She squeezed my hand. "The police are going to want you to tell them about it. They're looking for him."

"Seriously?" Everything was so confusing. So I decided to take another nap.

TWO DAYS WENT by before I felt even a little bit like myself. The nurses kept telling me that the body heals on its own time. Apparently I didn't have a lot of say over it. I kept drifting off in the middle of sentences. "You have a concussion, too," people kept telling me. "Take it easy."

As if I had a choice. My mother was like a dragon at the gates. She regulated who was allowed to see me and who was not. I had brief visits from Boz, who had apparently helped the EMTs carry me out of the woods to the waiting ambulance. Not that I remembered. "I guess I...owe you a case of beer?" I suggested. What did one get for the guy who'd hefted your broken body off the frozen pathway?

"At least," he said. "You're heavier than you look."

The ophthalmologist kept making return visits to check on my vision. I was having trouble focusing my right eye, and it freaked me right out. "I know the blurriness is odd, but that might be 20/20 a month from now," my female surgeon assured me more than once.

I wasn't blind, anyway. So that was something.

The other thing that freaked me out? Cax never came to see me, and nobody would tell me why. Each time I woke up from one of my many naps, I'd look around the room for him with my blurry vision.

He was never there.

CHAPTER TWENTY-ONE

Caxton

It was late—nine o'clock already. I had no idea if they'd let me see him, but I had to try. Room 412 was at the end of a long hall, and just knowing he was down there somewhere made me start to jog. Nobody stopped me.

I was afraid that Axel wasn't going to want a thing to do with me now, not after all the trouble I'd caused him. It would break my heart, but I'd understand. When he was well enough to leave the hospital I imagined that he'd go somewhere far away from here. Probably back to Ohio...

The door to room 412 was ajar, but it was completely quiet inside. The soft, yellow glow of lamplight shone on the walls. I nudged the door open and looked at the sleeping figure on the bed. Half his face was obscured by a big bandage, and the other half was bruised purple and green.

A sob pulsed in my throat. I clamped a hand over my mouth. What had I done?

Someone rose from the chair beside the bed. His mother. She looked exactly the same as I remembered from all those years ago. Yay—another person who surely hated me now. But when I braced myself to meet her eyes, I found her face soft-ening. "Cax," she whispered. "You look just the same."

Did I? I didn't feel the same.

"He's been waiting for you," she said.

My throat was twisted tight. "I've been…"

"I know," she said, resting a hand on my back. "You have a lot on your plate." To my surprise, she wrapped her arms around me and hugged me.

I just stood there feeling stunned. I almost got this woman's son killed, and now she was hugging me? "I'm sorry," I said.

She only held me tighter. "You've been through so much, you two. But it's going to get better now."

Was it? I wish I believed her.

Ms. Armitage stepped back, and I could see that her eyes were damp. "I'm going to go to his apartment to shower and sleep some. Can you stay a while?"

"A couple of hours," I whispered.

She nudged me toward the chair. "Sit. I'm going."

I sat and made myself take a good look at Axel—at the destruction I'd wrought. One arm was in a cast. His face was discolored and looked so very painful. He breathed peacefully enough in his sleep, though.

His good hand lay right there beside me, and I wanted to pick it up and kiss it. But I didn't do it. He needed his sleep. I'd done him enough harm already.

I leaned my elbows on the edge of the mattress and propped my head in my hands. I was so, so tired. It was hard to believe that I'd ever feel upbeat about anything again.

I must have nodded off. My head had sagged against the edge of the mattress. And now there was a warm hand sifting through my hair…

On a gasp, I sat up.

"Sorry," Axel whispered. "Couldn't help myself." He smiled at me.

The sight of that familiar smile set into his beat-up face made my eyes suddenly hot. I gulped back tears. "I'm so sorry," I said, my voice breaking. "You... I..."

His smile faded. "Don't cry. It's not as bad as it looks."

"It is, though." I grabbed his hand and held it in both of mine, kissing his palm. "He could have *killed* you!" A sob escaped my throat.

"But he didn't," Axel said quickly. "I'm still here. But for three days I've been wondering where you were. And nobody would talk about you. Where have you been?"

Tears ran down my face, and I swiped at them. "Well, after I got out of jail..."

"What?" Axel's good eye got round. "What the fuck?"

"Nobody told you about that?"

He shook his head a little and then winced. "No. Why were you in jail?"

"I got arrested for your assault. Because of that sexual harassment claim, they thought I might have..."

"Jesus," Axel gasped. "They asked me when I'd last seen you."

"Yeah. It was messy. And I was freaking out because my brothers were home alone. There was talk of sending Scotty to a foster home, because the asshole ran."

"Nobody told me any of this," Axel whispered, squeezing my hand. "I didn't know."

"I think they were trying not to scare you." I sighed. "Anyway, it took a day to straighten that out. They gave me a polygraph test and everything. I might still be in there if my father hadn't fled the state, making himself look guilty as fuck. When they let me out, I had to round up the boys and sort of half-explain why their father was apprehended in Connecticut and is now in jail. And then I had to find a family-law expert to be my lawyer."

"Jesus. Why?"

"Because I have to sue for custody of my brothers before my father gets out. His bail hearing was today. I went to it to testify against him."

"Holy shit," Axel said. "You have been busy. So..." His tired face creased with confusion. "Where is he now?"

"They caught him in Stamford, in a car he'd rented with cash. The rental agent called the cops when she saw his face on TV."

"TV?"

"Yep. Manhunt. Anyway, he's in the county jail. He was denied bail, thank God. Otherwise I'd be in a real panic right now, hoping he didn't show up to scare me away from the boys. He actually yelled at me in court today. 'Keep the pervert away from my sons.'"

"Oh baby, I'm sorry. You don't need that."

I shook my head. "Don't be sorry. He only made himself look crazier. My lawyer is fast-tracking my petition for full custody. We don't know what kind of sentence he's going to receive for hurting you. So I have to be ready."

"God damn." Axel took a deep breath and blew it out. "Your life is blowing up all over the place."

"Yes and no." I kissed his hand again. What I really wanted was to climb in bed with him and hold him tight. And I'd do that if I could be sure I wouldn't hurt him. "I always wanted to take care of my brothers. I think I'm going to get that chance. And as long as you're okay, then nothing else matters."

Axel regarded me sleepily. "I'm okay." His eyes fluttered closed.

"Ax? I'm going to have to go home soon. I'm sorry. But I'll come back tomorrow when Scotty is at school."

"Okay," he mumbled.

"I love you," I whispered to the sleeping man in the bed. Tomorrow he'd probably think things over and realize that the almost-boyfriend who almost got him killed was now a parent to three kids. And he'd realize that I wasn't ever going to live the fun lifestyle that a young, gay man should enjoy.

That kind of life just wasn't in the cards for me.

But as long as Axel recovered, I was going to be okay. When he moved on to someone with less baggage, my heart would break. But I would survive. I'd have to.

CHAPTER TWENTY-TWO

Axel

After I got out of the hospital, my mother and I spent several days cooped up in my little apartment. Mostly I lay around watching TV and popping aspirin. Once, Mom and I went downstairs to Josh and Caleb's for dinner. But I'm ashamed to say that a couple hours sitting up and being social tired me out.

A couple of times I talked to Cax on the phone for a few minutes. The last time, I'd timed it badly, catching him when he was trying to fix a meal for his brothers. "I really need some cooking lessons," he whispered into the phone. "I'm making entire meals out of stuff from the frozen foods aisle."

I stopped short of offering to come over and help, because I was afraid he'd refuse. Cax had some major family issues to work through. I could only imagine what The Month Dad Went to Jail was like for Scotty and his older brothers.

Also, I was pretty sure Cax hadn't told them about me.

The following week I started feeling a lot better. "You need to get home," I told my mother.

"I know," she said with a sigh. Mom was a high school

teacher, and she'd already taken an unholy number of personal days. "Do you want to come with me?"

"No," I said immediately. But then I took a second to think about it. I wasn't expected back at work for another week or two, depending on how I was healing up. And Cax and I had reverted to email as our primary means of communication. With his brothers' needs and my lack of privacy, there just wasn't time or opportunity to talk on the phone, let alone see each other.

But in the end, I decided to stay on in Massachusetts.

Mom finally left after making me promise to call her every day. "I will. God."

She kissed me for the hundredth time and finally got into a cab to the airport.

That afternoon, Josh and Caleb dropped by. "You could come with us tonight for dinner at Maggie and Daniel's," Caleb offered.

"Maggie is a caterer. The food always rocks." Josh winked.

But I wasn't feeling it. I was lonely and in a funk and I preferred to sulk by myself. "Thanks, but I'm going to bed early."

The next few days were cold and dreary. I watched too much television and ate a lot of homemade soup that my mother had cooked and frozen before she'd left.

Twice each day—like clockwork—someone stopped by to visit me. I was positive they'd scheduled it that way. Josh was always one of my visitors. Sometimes Boz came by, and once my boss Arnie brought me a meal of fast-food chicken. That was nice and all, but I missed Cax.

Even Jason came to visit me. He brought take-out cheeseburgers from Bruisers and a six pack. "I heard you were going to miss a couple of intramural basketball games," he said. "So I brought the bar to you."

"That is really, really nice of you," I said, touched.

"Well..." He grinned at me. "When I asked you out, you said you were hung up on someone. I guess I can work out who that is now."

"Can you?" I teased. "You must read the newspaper."

He nodded, biting his lip. "I asked Cax once if he was gay, and he made a face like I'd just accused him of being an ax murderer. At the time I got kind of offended. But now I get it."

I took a bite of my burger before answering. "Cax spent a lot of years trying not to get the shit kicked out of him by his dad."

"But then you got his beating instead."

"Yeah. I knew the guy was pretty crazy. But I didn't see it coming."

He flinched. "Sorry, man. Dating me woulda been simpler."

I laughed, then lifted my beer to toast him. "Hindsight is clearer than the vision in my right eye." Jason made a sad face, but I waved it off. "Gallows humor, man. And I'll be jumping past you on the court in no time. That's what they tell me."

He smiled. "We'll just see about that. Can I tell you something funny? You're the first guy I ever asked out."

"What?" I yelped through a mouthful. After swallowing, I asked for clarification. "How is that possible?"

"The thing about crazy families is that they come in all flavors." He toyed with the straw in his soda. "My family is never going to put anyone in the hospital. But they have other ways of trying to control me. I'm twenty-five years old, and I've never dated anyone."

Holy shit. "Holy shit," I said aloud. "And I thought Cax was sheltered."

"I hook up," he said, his face reddening. "But I don't date. Or I haven't yet. It's complicated. My family spent a lot of effort trying to convince me I was just confused. And I did my undergraduate degree at one of those colleges where you can get kicked out for acting on same-sex attraction."

"Ouch." I studied Jason's handsome features and wondered how someone so friendly and so attractive had never had a boyfriend. He was too preppy to be my type, but still wildly attractive, with golden skin and long eyelashes. A pretty boy. "Then I'm sorry the first time you asked someone out, he said no."

"I'm not. Seriously." Jason smiled again, revealing a set of perfect teeth. "Because the world didn't end when you said no. It made me wonder what I'd been so afraid of."

"You shouldn't be afraid. You're smart and attractive and not an asshole. Not many people are going to turn that down."

"We'll see." He crumpled up his hamburger wrapper. "Isn't there a basketball game on?"

I WAS STILL WAITING for the visitor I really wanted to see. When I talked with Cax on the phone again, I learned that his brothers were on winter vacation, and he was spending a lot of time with them.

The following Saturday I couldn't take my isolation any longer. It took me about fifteen minutes to get my coat on over my broken arm. I wiggled my feet into my hiking boots so that I wouldn't have to untie and retie them. And I managed a hat and mittens.

I left a note on the door. *Nobody panic. I went for a walk.* Whoever was on Axel Duty that day would probably find it before I got back. The last thing I did was to slip my phone into my coat pocket.

Outside, I found that it had snowed a few inches

overnight. *Fuck.* Someone—Josh probably—had already shoveled the stairs down from my apartment. But the sidewalks were going to be tricky to navigate. I hated feeling so awkward and fragile. But I was not about to turn around.

Carefully, I made my way down the stairs. I took a look at the path through the woods. The snow had blown into drifts there. It looked passable, but difficult. *Damn. It. All.* I hated being injured. Worse yet, I hated that I was a little wary of walking through the park. I knew Mr. Williams was behind bars. But he'd made me afraid. And I'd never been afraid before.

Chin up, Armitage, I coached myself. I turned around and went the other way—down Newbury Street. The road had been plowed, but half the sidewalks were still buried.

I would just have to walk in the street.

I'd made it to the end of Newbury Street when a Toyota approached, then stopped at the curb. The window lowered and Caleb stuck his head out. "Whatcha doing?"

"Taking a walk."

Caleb frowned. "I know that sometimes the point of taking a walk is to *walk*. But is there anywhere I could drop you?"

I only hesitated for a second. "Yeah, if you don't mind. It isn't far."

"Get in."

FIVE MINUTES LATER, we slowed to a stop outside the Williams house. Cax's car was in the snowy drive. "Thank you," I said.

"Will you call me if you need a ride home?" he asked

quietly. "You don't want to get in trouble with Josh. He might start checking on you *four* times a day."

I laughed. "Okay. I hope I won't need a ride, though."

Caleb regarded me thoughtfully. "I hope you won't, too. But don't give up. I waited years to be with Josh. And it was worth it."

Wow. "I guess I'll try to be patient."

He grinned. "Call me if you need a lift, though. It's, like, a seven-minute drive."

"I promise."

After Caleb drove away, I picked my way up the snowy driveway and knocked on what must be the kitchen door.

A few seconds later the door was yanked open by Scotty. "Hi!" he said cheerily. "What happened to your face?"

My good hand flew to my cheekbone, as if covering my scar would make it go away. It hadn't occurred to me that I'd have to answer that question. Cax had told the boys that their father was in jail for attacking someone, but he hadn't told them who. "I had a bit of an accident," I lied. "It looks worse than it is."

"Bummer!" Scotty opened the door all the way, making room for me.

I stepped into a kitchen that opened onto a family room. The kitchen hadn't been updated in a long time, but it was a good size, with a comfortable dining table. A teenage boy sat at the table reading the comics page from the newspaper. In the habit of teenage boys everywhere, he didn't even look up when I entered. With his dark, bushy hair, he looked more like his father than like Cax.

In the family room stood a third boy, the middle one—he wasn't a child like Scotty, but neither was he man-sized like his big brother. His eyes tracked me as I entered the room. But he didn't stop eating the piece of toast he was busy cramming into his mouth.

"Mark!" Cax's voice scolded from nearby. "Eat that in the kitchen. Or at least get a plate. The drill sergeant may not be here to march us around, but we can't turn into slobs."

Mark shoved the last of the toast into his mouth and brushed the crumbs off his hands, rendering the discussion moot.

Cax made an ornery sound and then came into view. He stopped short when he saw me, his face opening up into surprise.

"Hi," I said.

He took a step toward me and then stopped. He opened his mouth and then closed it again. "Hi," he said eventually.

"Um, I just…" *I just shouldn't have come.*

As I watched, Cax gathered himself together. He started toward me again. "Cup of coffee? I just made a pot."

"I'd love one. Thanks."

"Let me take your coat."

"Well…" That wasn't as easy as it looked. "Give me a second." I felt eyes on me as I fumbled with the zipper on my coat. I slid out my left arm with no trouble. But getting it off my broken arm required more effort.

"Here," Cax said, moving closer. "Let me." He lifted the weight of the coat off my shoulder and eased the sleeve off my cast.

We were standing very close. Lazy Saturday whiskers lay over his jaw, and I longed to lean forward and measure their roughness with my lips.

His gaze lifted to mine, and I saw longing there. The corners of his mouth twitched, too. But he said nothing. He only reached up to remove the hat from my head. "That's better. Now let's get you some coffee."

It wasn't until he turned away that I felt all the eyes on me. Mark, the toast-monster, was watching me with a grim expression. And the comic-reading teen was staring with undisguised curiosity. "Who broke your arm?" he asked suddenly.

Well, fuck. I looked to Cax for help, but his back was to me as he reached into a cabinet for coffee mugs. "Jared," he said softly. "Not now."

"It was Dad, wasn't it?" Mark asked suddenly.

"Why would Dad break Axel's arm?" Scotty asked. "Is Dad in jail for *hurting Axel?*" He finished the question on a squeak.

Slowly, Cax turned around. He held a mug of coffee in each hand. He took a sip from one of them before he spoke. "Dad didn't like Axel very much, but I do. Because Axel is my boyfriend."

There was a deep silence, and I checked everyone's faces. Scotty was blinking at me, as if trying to do the math. Jared— the teen at the table—looked as if he'd just tasted something bitter.

But it was Mark who looked truly horrified. "What the *fuck?*"

"Mark, don't use that word," Cax said automatically.

"What the actual fuck," Mark spat, ignoring him. "You're..." He turned to Cax, and I braced myself. I knew what was coming. "A faggot? My brother is a *faggot*."

The other f-word. So much worse than the first one he'd used.

All the color drained from Cax's face. "You *watch your mouth*," he threatened. Cax had a really easy-going personality. But I was pretty sure I was about to see what happened when he snapped.

I didn't get the chance, because Mark shot out of the room toward the front of the house. I heard a scuffle, the thunk of a pair of shoes, and then the sound of the front door opening. It shut with a bone-shaking slam a moment later.

Jared got up from the table. Giving me wide berth, as if I might be contagious, he left the room. Another door slammed somewhere else in the house.

That left Scotty. With his eyes still on me, he moved. He didn't turn or run. Instead, he inched closer to Cax, sidling against him the way a frightened fawn moves closer to its mother.

Cax's face was still white. He stood like a statue, holding the two cups of coffee.

I took a couple of steps forward and relieved him of one of them. He wrapped his now free hand around Scotty's shoulders. "I'm sorry your brothers are freaking out right now," he said to him quietly.

"But why are they?" Scotty asked.

Cax met my eyes with something like wonder on his face. Why indeed? How did you explain ignorance and prejudice to someone who seemed not to understand it? "Well..." He took a deep breath. "I surprised them, I think. They didn't know that I had a boyfriend."

"Oh." Scotty's small face was frowning, as if he still couldn't make sense of it.

"Look," Cax said, gesturing with his mug. "Sit down on the sofa. We need to get Axel off his feet." He gave Scotty a nudge toward the family room.

Scotty trotted toward the cozier seating area.

"I should go," I said.

"No." Cax gave me a wan smile. "I wish you wouldn't. I mean..." He sighed. "This might have gone better. But I've been avoiding you because I didn't know how to tell them. I guess I don't need to worry about that anymore."

"But…" I sighed. "You have to deal with the fallout now. I'm just in the way."

His eyes pleaded with me. "Please don't walk out that door. There's way too much of that in our lives. I don't want you to be uncomfortable, but…"

"Okay," I whispered.

He reached up and touched the mostly healed side of my face. "Come sit."

I followed Cax over to the generous sofa. He sat down in the middle, and Scotty moved immediately to sit close to him. Cax dropped an arm over his littlest brother's skinny shoulders.

Lowering myself carefully so that I wouldn't jostle my arm, I sat in the opposite corner, leaving some space between Cax and me. I appreciated that he was willing to have me around, but I didn't want anyone to feel weird.

"Where do you think Mark went?" Scotty asked.

"To a friend's house, probably," Cax said. "If we don't hear from him in a couple of hours, I'll call around."

Scotty was silent a minute. "Amy wasn't really your girl-friend," he said. "I never saw you kiss her. Not like a *real* kiss."

Cax chuckled. "You are smarter than your brothers. Did you know that?"

Scotty's grin lasted about one second. Then his smooth brow wrinkled again. "Why did Dad break Axel's arm? Why is Mark being a douche?"

"Don't say…"

"Douche," Scotty interjected. "I know. Just answer the question."

I tried to hide my smile behind my coffee mug, but it wasn't easy. Man, Scotty killed me. What a great kid.

"There are just some people in the world who don't think

it's okay for a guy to have a boyfriend. I don't have a better explanation than that. Because there isn't one."

"Dad didn't like Axel?"

"Dad didn't even *know* Axel. He just hated the idea of Axel and I together. See, Axel and I were friends in Ohio. And then I didn't see him for a long time..." Cax turned his head to give me a little smile. "But then he moved here to work for the athletic department. And when Dad saw him that day I had the headache, he kind of flipped out."

"Not *kind of*," Scotty scoffed. "He had a major freak attack."

"Yeah, and I'm sorry," Cax said softly. "It's not what I wanted for you. Or Axel."

Scotty made a grumpy noise in his throat. "Is it awful that I'm glad he's gone and you're here? There's no one screaming at us anymore."

I saw Cax close his eyes. He leaned back on the sofa, his little brother's head resting against his shoulder. "You aren't awful, Scotty. You could never be awful."

We were all quiet for a minute. I sipped my coffee, feeling self-conscious. But Cax's hand reached across the sofa, finding the fingers of my broken arm where they protruded from my cast. He held them gently.

"Cax?" Scotty asked.

"Yeah?"

"Would now be a good time to ask you if I could watch the newest Avengers movie? It just hit Netflix."

Cax chuckled. "Sure, kid. Turn it on."

Scotty pointed the remote at the TV and began to click around, looking for his movie. When he found it, Cax let go of my hand and stood. "You need anything?" he asked me.

I shook my head.

"I'm going to try to talk to Jared." He walked behind the sofa, then paused, his hand in my hair.

"Cool," Scotty said, his eyes on the fight scene that opened the movie.

Cax leaned down and placed a silent kiss on the top of my head. Then he left the room.

"Who's your favorite Avenger?" Scotty asked.

It took me a second to realize that I was the target of the question, because the kid's eyes never left the screen. "Thor," I said quickly.

"Not Iron Man? Really? Why?"

"I like his, um, hammer," I said, then inwardly snickered. Thor was my favorite because I wanted to lick Chris Hemsworth's sixpack. But the kid didn't need to know that.

"Cool," Scotty said, his small face pointed right at the screen.

I took another sip of coffee while the movie lit the room. A surprising contentment settled over me, and even Scotty gave a happy sigh.

CHAPTER TWENTY-THREE

Caxton

I knocked on Jared's door, but there was no response.

Typical.

"Jared." I tapped again. Then I tried the knob and the door opened.

My brother was lying on his bed, earbuds in, staring at the ceiling. His gaze jerked toward me, and I braced myself to see disgust on his face.

There wasn't any, though. I saw only the teenage reluctance I was used to seeing. He took the earbuds out.

I closed the door behind me and sat on his neglected desk chair. "I just want to say a couple of things."

He nodded and sat up. For Jared, that was practically rolling out the rug for me.

"I know I never said anything before, but I've always been gay." He flinched a little, but I soldiered on. "You're probably shocked, but try to remember that I'm still the same guy you always call when you have a problem. I'm the same guy who shoots hoops with you in the driveway."

"I know," he said, his voice rough.

He did? I waited to see where that went. Unfortunately, he didn't say another word. "Look, Dad never had any nice things to say about gay men. Or black men. Or..."

"I *know* that," Jared argued. "That's not me, though, okay? I'm not like that."

Studying him, I tried to decide what that meant. If he was trying to tell me that he was okay with it, I wasn't sure I believed him. He didn't look okay. At the risk of getting my head snapped off, I asked, "Then what's with the long face?"

Jared rolled his eyes. "I miss Amy, okay? I hoped she'd be back."

"Oh," I said slowly. "The thing is..." I cleared my throat. "Amy and I weren't really together. She has a boyfriend—a nice guy she met at work."

Jared winced. "Shit."

"Yeah. But she hasn't, like, left the country or anything. I could have her over for dinner this week." The truth was that I hadn't told her any of my recent troubles. I'd been trying to give her space. She'd covered my ass for so long that I hadn't wanted to drag her down into the latest disasters.

"I suppose," Jared said with a sigh. "But it won't be the same. She is..." He swallowed. "She was, like..." He looked away.

And all of a sudden I understood what he could not possibly say out loud, and it was just as sad as everything else that had happened this month. "It's that she mothered us a little, didn't she? Me included."

Jared's eyes snapped to mine, but he didn't dare agree with me, because he couldn't give a voice to an ache that big.

Of all of us, I'd had the most time with our mother. Jared had been twelve when she'd died—about Scotty's age now. And Scotty had been in kindergarten.

After she'd died, I'd learned to live with that heartache. But I hadn't realized how my brothers couldn't really do that.

Lately, I'd been so wrapped up in my father's shortcomings that I hadn't stopped to wonder what motherlessness was like for Jared.

My eyes filled unexpectedly. There were so many gaps in my brothers' lives, and I was never going to be able to fill them all.

Jared turned his chin away, but not quickly enough for me to miss the single tear that rolled down his face. I had a decision to make. Hug him, or not? Usually, he'd rather die than receive my affection. But, Goddamn it, maybe this wasn't one of those times.

I compromised.

Crossing the room in three paces, I sat down on the bed beside him. I put both hands on the back of his shoulders and squeezed. "I'm sorry about Amy. But it wasn't real between us," I whispered. "I don't have it in me, and she knew that."

He dropped his head, but leaned back a fraction of an inch into my touch.

I massaged his skinny shoulders and sighed. "Would you do me a favor? Amy is, like, two weeks out of date on all the crazy stuff happening around here. Would you mind calling her and getting her up to speed? I should do it myself, but I'm kind of embarrassed."

He turned his head to look at me. "Really?"

"Yeah. She's going to kill me when she hears all the crap we've been through, and the fact that we didn't ask her for help."

One corner of Jared's mouth twitched. That was as much enthusiasm as I'd seen from him in a year. "Where's your phone?"

~

I LEFT Jared alone to call Amy. Since Axel and Scotty were deep into their movie, I went into the kitchen to clean up. Depending on what she had planned for today, I expected to be Amy-bombed either five minutes from now or whenever her schedule allowed.

When I thought about it, I realized how weird it was that I hadn't heard from her these past ten days. My father's arrest had been all over the local newspaper. Even if Amy eschewed the *Berkshire Valley Times* in favor of the *Boston Globe*, someone would have mentioned it to her.

I tried to remember the last time I'd talked to her. Amy had checked in with me right before Axel's attack. And then... nothing. That was downright weird, and it gave me a prickle of worry. Had I missed something that had happened to her? Jeez, I hoped not. But my bandwidth was seriously strained at the moment.

"Cax?"

I turned to see Jared leaning on the fridge. He set my phone down and frowned. "Did you get Amy?"

He nodded, looking grim. "Mark is with her, actually."

"Really?" I tossed the sponge on the counter. "Is everyone okay?"

Jared shrugged. "She says he's not ready to come home."

"Okay. Should I, uh, call her?"

He shook his head. "She said she'll come over later. Around suppertime." He turned to go.

That made me feel helpless. "Well, I guess I'd better figure out something for supper."

Jared looked over his shoulder again. "Oh—Amy said she and Mark would bring dinner."

I laughed. "Of course she did."

In the living room, Scotty was glued to the screen, but Axel had dozed off. I grabbed a Barmuth College throw blanket and covered him with it, taking a moment to admire the way his dark lashes swept down toward his cheekbones. Then I sat down beside Scotty to watch the rest of his movie with him.

∾

AFTER THE MOVIE, Axel woke up. Scotty ran off to the computer to try to figure out when the next Avengers film would come out.

I went into the kitchen to get us a couple of sodas. As I poured the Coke over ice cubes, I couldn't believe how trippy it was to have Axel sitting in the family room. This was a day that I thought would never come. Even if things were horribly complicated, and one of my brothers wasn't speaking to me, it was still important to me.

I loved Axel, and I wanted him in my life. And everyone was just going to have to get used to it.

When I carried our drinks into the family room, Axel was texting someone. "Who are you talking to? Wait, that sounded jealous."

He chuckled. "It's Josh. He wants to know if I need a ride home. He and Caleb keep tabs on my movements. They're almost worse than my mother."

My chest got tight. It should have been me who'd helped him all week. But I'd been here, putting meals on the table, trying to convince my brothers that their lives weren't falling apart just because their father was now notorious for assault. "Tell Josh that I'll drive you home."

"I already did." He tried to shove his phone in his pocket, but then dropped it. "Fucking cast," he said.

"Don't say 'fucking,'" Scotty said, walking into the room. "Amy's car just pulled up."

I shot to my feet, but then thought better of rushing to

meet them. Wherever Mark's head was right now, it wouldn't help if I rushed him like an offensive lineman. I sat back down again and sipped my drink.

Both Axel and Scotty looked at me like I was nuts.

"Hello?" Amy called from the back door. "Cax?"

I stood up again and went toward the kitchen. "Hi."

Amy scurried to meet me halfway, so she could chew me out in relative privacy. "Cax? How do I not get a call when your father lands in prison? And you're suing the state for custody of your brothers?"

"I'm sorry," I whispered.

"*Jesus*, Cax. I was in Florida with Derek until yesterday. This morning my father tells me about the whole disaster. So I'm in my car driving over here to rip you a new one when Mark comes running out of the house like it's on fire..."

"Wait!" I held up a hand. "Back up. You were in Florida with Derek for *ten days?* Amy—that's not a vacation, that's cohabitation. Should I check the mailbox for a wedding announcement?"

She shoved my chest, and I grinned. I'd missed this. I'd missed *her*. "Don't interrupt me when I'm yelling at you," she snarled. But she was smiling, too.

Mark stomped into the back door with two bags of groceries. He set them down without looking at me. Then he went back outside again. "Um...?" I looked pointedly at the back door.

Amy pushed my chest again until she'd backed me all the way into the family room.

"Where's his head?" I whispered.

She flinched. "He's been taking a lot of crap from his friends about your father getting locked up. Damn social media. He wasn't invited to a couple of ski trips this past week and a party."

"He didn't tell me that," I whispered.

"I know. He's been trying to 'be a man,' whatever that means. But in his mind, you and Axel just make more fodder for gossip. He knows he was an asshole today, but he's not quite ready to get over himself. Your dad fed him a lot of homophobic crap, you know."

"Oh, I know," I sighed.

"Give him a little time."

"Okay."

"Meanwhile, let's talk about how you're a terrible friend. Where was my phone call? Your dad's in jail, your boyfriend's in the hospital and you're a single parent to three. How am I not notified?"

"Because you were in Florida with *Derrrrrrek*."

She pinched me. I tickled her.

"Ahem." Axel cleared his throat.

Amy took her hands off me. "Um. Hi! Sorry."

Axel grinned. "You must be Amy."

"Yeah." She hustled over to the sofa to shake his hand. "I don't usually pinch your boyfriend."

"I think he had it coming."

Amy grinned, then sat down beside Axel. "You know, Cax. He was cuter before your dad beat the crap out of him."

"Jesus," I gasped. "That's not funny."

But Axel and Amy were both laughing. "Gallows humor, Cax," Amy protested.

"I adore gallows humor," Axel agreed. He put his hands to his chest. "But laughing hurts."

"Aw. Poor baby." Amy patted Axel's arm.

The sight of two people I loved smiling at each other was almost more than I could bear. I wanted this so badly—a boyfriend, a family and friends. I wanted us to sit under one roof and have dinner together.

Which reminded me. "At the risk of sounding like the biggest jackass in the world..."

"What's for dinner?" Amy guessed.

"Well, Jared said something about food."

She grabbed my hand and pulled me down on the couch beside her. "Yes, my helpless one. I'm making chicken pad Thai." Then she dropped her voice. "I gave Mark the job of putting all the groceries away. It's keeping him busy for a few minutes so he can just ease his way back in here, okay? Let him come to you."

I kissed Amy on the nose. "Thank you. Where would I be without you?"

"Hungry, that's where. Now who's going to chop red peppers and peanuts for me?"

"I'll do it," Axel volunteered. "I can prep vegetables one-handed."

"Do you cook?" Amy asked. She jumped up and offered him a hand.

"Sure," he said, standing up slowly. "Doesn't everybody?"

"Everybody but Cax."

"He'll have to learn now," Axel said. "He has three kids to feed."

"We'll have some fun teaching him," Amy agreed.

I followed my two favorite people into the kitchen so they could tease me some more.

CHAPTER TWENTY-FOUR

Axel

Cax's brother Mark snuck looks at me all through dinner.

I never made eye contact, because I didn't think he'd want me to. I couldn't imagine the emotions he was dealing with. His father put a lot of shit in his head and then got hauled off to jail.

He'd come around, though. He was young, and Cax was good to him. Even though I'd watched the kid say awful things to Cax, my boyfriend was gentle to Mark at the dinner table. It practically broke my heart to see the tenderness he had for his brothers. All the sacrifices he'd made to stay close to his family made sense to me now that I could see it firsthand.

Amy helped, too. She was upbeat and fun, and it was easy to see how well the boys liked her. She was awesome. I felt not a shred of lover's jealousy that she'd once slept with Cax. Instead, I was just happy to know he'd had someone like Amy on his side all these years. She made his past seem less grim.

We ate her delicious cooking together, and the boys cleared the table. Then Amy dug a pack of cards out of her purse and began to shuffle. "Who's dealing the first poker game?"

All three of Cax's brothers wanted in. So I anted up a few of the plastic poker chips that Scotty had run to find, and played a hand. But after a few minutes I became ridiculously tired.

Cax noticed without my having to say anything. "I'm going to take you home now," he said, pushing back his chair.

"Nice meeting you, Axel," Amy said, shuffling the cards.

"Likewise." I got up and looked around for my coat.

"Actually," Cax said, clearing his throat. "I'm going to make sure Axel's walkway has been shoveled. It snowed again today. So I might be a little while."

"Yep," Amy said without looking up. "You take care of that walkway. I'll tell Scotty when it's time for bed." Cax left the room without a word. Amy looked up at me and winked.

"Goodnight," I said to everyone.

"Night!" Scotty yelled, reaching for his cards.

Jared muttered something that was probably "goodnight." And Mark said nothing.

"YOU KNOW Josh shovels my steps, right?" I said as Cax and I motored toward my apartment.

"I'm counting on it," he said. "Because I needed a little time alone with you. Do you have groceries? Are you really okay?" He shook his head. "I hate that you're alone. I'd ask you to stay with us but..."

"I'm fine," I said softly. "Really."

He parked beside Caleb's Toyota and walked me up the stairs. They'd been shoveled to perfection, of course.

Inside, he helped me out of my coat, his eyes warm. "I love you," he whispered. "I'm sorry it's been way too long since I said it in person."

196

I stepped into his body and hugged him with my good arm. "It's okay, Cax. Everything is going to be okay."

"Is it?" He squeezed me around the waist. "My life is a giant mess right now."

I shook my head, my nose landing at his neck. "That's not really true. Precarious, maybe. But things are about to get better."

"Are they? I have to give up on my PhD and find a real job."

Stepping back, I looked into his eyes. "Fuck, why?"

"I don't own that house," he said. "It's my father's mortgage. And he can't pay it if he's in jail. I'm just a starving grad student. Can't keep three kids in burgers and Nikes on a teaching-assistant gig."

Hugging him again, I made a sad sound in the back of my throat. "Please don't move away. Because then I'll need to find a new job wherever you are. And that won't be easy."

His body went very still against mine, and his voice was hesitant. "I don't know what the future holds."

"I do." I gave him a squeeze. "It holds you. Because we did not just get through all this bullshit with your father to let something like a job get in our way."

Cax took a deep, shuddery breath and laid his head on my shoulder. "When you say it like that, I almost believe it."

"You should believe it, because you're mine. You've always been mine, and I'm not giving you up."

He smiled into my jaw line. "You wouldn't really quit your Barmuth job if I had to move to Boston."

I gave him a kiss on the ear. "There's a story I need to tell you. But we have to sit down." Cax let me lead him over to my sofa. It was the first time we'd ever sat there together, but I hoped it wouldn't be the last. "I got the Barmuth job offer through a Skype interview and a recommendation at OSU."

He nodded, his hand gently skimming the fingertips that protruded from my cast.

"When I was trying to figure out whether or not I wanted to move here and take the job, I watched a Barmuth basketball game. I streamed it on some college sports network. And on camera, I saw you sitting in your seats. I recognized you."

Cax's mouth fell open. "No fucking way," he breathed.

"Way," I said with a chuckle. "I wasn't ever going to say anything, because it sounds so stalkerish. But part of the reason I came all the way to Barmuth was you."

"God, Ax." His eyes brimmed. "That's crazy."

"I know."

He shook his head. "I mean it's crazy that you *found* me. And that you'd look in the first place."

Something shifted in my chest. "I'll always look for you, baby. Please don't worry about money and jobs. We'll figure it out. Your father might be ordered to pay support. He can sell that house and pay it out of his equity. And you and I can buy some other place. I make money. Not a ton—but it's a living."

Cax's eyes widened. "You would...buy a house with me?"

Hadn't he been listening? "Any day of the week."

He leaned back against the sofa and closed his eyes. "I'm afraid to feel happy. Like, if I let my guard down, something else will come along to screw me."

"That would be me."

He opened his eyes and smiled. "Not tonight, though. Not until you stop making that pain face when you move around."

"I hope it's soon, then."

He patted my leg. "Let's get you tucked into bed. Do you need anything first? A shower? Help with your kitchen?"

I eyed my bathroom door. "I could use a shower. It's so awkward holding my arm out of the curtain. Could you hand me the shampoo?"

"Any day of the week," he said with a smile.

Cax did even better than that. He helped me out of my clothes. That was sexy in a frustrating way, because nothing would come of it tonight. Then he set up the shower and held my hand as I stepped in, supporting my broken arm as I stood under the spray.

"Ahh," I said. "It's been taking me like a half hour just to get to this point alone."

"I'm always available to undress you," he joked. And then we were both silent, wishing it was actually true.

Cax did better than hand me the shampoo. He tossed his own shirt out the bathroom door, then reached into the shower and lathered up my hair. He let his hands skim my neck and shoulders. I lifted my arms to be washed there, too. He went for another little pump of soap, then let out a sexy growl while he spread suds along my belly, my hips, my ass.

My groin.

"Okay." He sighed. "That was just gratuitous. Sorry."

I chuckled. "Sorry you stopped?"

Cax groaned. "Rinse off before I climb in there with you."

Even though that sounded like a fun idea, I obeyed.

After the shower came the towel. Cax dried my body gently while I held my cast away from my wet skin. He dabbed at my back, then kissed my damp skin. He dried my legs, his face close enough to my groin to give me a semi.

Groaning, he got to his feet, and I saw that he was tenting his pants.

"There isn't enough sex in this relationship," I mumbled.

"No kidding," he agreed, swiping water droplets off my collarbone. "Lean forward so that I can dry your hair."

When I'd passed inspection, I padded out of the bathroom and over to my bed while Cax fetched me a fresh pair of briefs from my dresser. He knelt down in front of me, still bare-chested, holding the elastic waist open for me to step into. But before I could, his eyes raised to mine. The hungry look in them made me hard.

He licked his lips. "I have a parting gift for you before I go."

"Mmm?" I said, distracted by the proximity of his mouth to my dick.

"Sit down," he said, tossing the briefs aside.

The second my ass landed on the bed, he pressed his hands down on either side of my thighs. Then he dipped his head and took me in his mouth.

"Oh," I gasped. "So *good*."

And it was. He swirled his tongue around my cockhead, then deep-throated me on the first try.

"Fuuuuuck," I panted. "You are getting *very* good at this. Who've you been practicing on? I'm going to kick his ass."

Cax chuckled around my dick, then popped off, pumping me with his hand. "Just my imagination and slutty videos." He kissed my tip, and then took me deep.

And, *ungh!* It had been a long time since we were together. And I'd been too ill and tired to get myself off. Suddenly, a lot of pent up lust began tightening up my balls. My hips rolled, and I was approaching the finish line a heck of a lot faster than usual. "Whew," I panted, stroking his hair with my good hand. "This isn't going to take long."

"Mmm," he moaned around my cock, and the vibrations made me crazy. I gripped his hair more tightly in my hand. "Caxy..." I choked out. He gave me a good, hard suck and then I was coming. "Baby," I gasped, erupting in his mouth.

He swallowed, then swallowed again. I had to let go of his hair and plant my hand on the bed, because I was suddenly feeling dizzy. I tipped my head back and practically melted onto the comforter.

Meanwhile, Cax started laughing. Then he ran into my bathroom and I heard the water running.

"Did I choke you?" I asked when the water shut off.

He chuckled. "Let's not forget that I'm a newbie." He emerged, smiling. "But that was a porn-star load."

"Jesus." I grinned at the ceiling. "Felt like one. It's been a while." Even more than I loved coming like a freight train, I loved that we were laughing right now. There'd been way too much drama between us, and I think I'd needed this moment of levity more than I needed the blowjob.

He walked over and bent down, kissing my forehead. "I have to go home."

"I know. But don't I get to return the favor?"

He kissed me on the lips and straightened. "Not this time. But I promise to think of you later while I'm soaping up my dick in the shower."

"Wish I could be there."

He pulled me to a sitting position with my good hand. "Now get under the covers. I'll call you tomorrow."

"Okay." I let him tuck me in. "Love you, Cax."

"Love you more," he said.

I doubted that could be true. But I sure liked hearing it.

CHAPTER TWENTY-FIVE

Caxton

Ten days after I came out to my brothers, I stood in a courtroom listening to the judge appoint me temporary emergency custody of all three of them. The judge banged his gavel once on the bench—just like in the movies—and I felt my eyes get wet.

Too bad the boys weren't there to hear it. They were back in school. And my father wasn't there to hear it, because he was in jail.

But Axel was there. When I turned around, I saw him waiting in the back of the room, his smile bright on his face—the bruises were fading, thank God.

My lawyer babbled at my side as I walked toward the exit doors. "Temporary custody is just a formality. He won't get the kids back," he promised.

"Thank you," I mumbled. All I could see was Axel's smile. When I reached him, he hugged me.

It took me a second to hug him back, because old habits die hard. I didn't know how long it would take me to forget to be afraid—to forget all the years I'd hidden myself. But after a moment, the good times won out over the bad. I hugged him hard, because his ribs weren't hurting him much anymore. And because I didn't care who saw us.

"I want to take you out for coffee," he said.

"All right," I agreed. "Can we swing by my library carrel? I need my books if I'm going to blow off the afternoon."

"Anything you need."

Smiling, I took his hand and walked him toward the parking lot. Because all I *really* needed was him.

When we got to the graduate library, Axel came inside with me. Again, I had to fight off a shiver of worry. *It doesn't matter*, I reminded myself. *Anyone can know. It's okay*. I held the door for him, then put a hand to his back as we walked down the hall. I was sick of hiding. I was done with it.

And when Jason appeared in the atrium, walking toward us, that was okay, too. "Hi," Axel said, my palm still at the small of his back. "How've you been?"

Jason looked from me to Axel and back again. "Just fine. You?"

"It's been a rough month," Axel said with a chuckle. "But things are looking up."

Jason cleared his throat. "I can see that."

"Hey," I broke in. But then there was silence, because I didn't know how to proceed. He'd asked me if I was gay, and I'd lied about it. "I, uh. It's..."

Jason shook his head. "Don't worry about it. I read the papers." He winked. "Seems like you were in a tough spot."

"That's one way to put it," I said, and Axel laughed. "We're getting some coffee," I added. "Care to join us?"

Jason's lips twitched. "You two go ahead. Maybe another time." He walked away smiling.

"We have to find a nice guy for him," Axel said when he was gone.

"Totally. And soon."

When we got outside again, I asked Axel where he wanted to go.

"I'll show you," he said. "But let's take your car."

"Okay." Since he was still a bit fragile, the request to go by car didn't seem weird. But then he began directing me into a residential neighborhood. Then he asked me to turn down Newbury Street.

"I think I like this coffee shop," I said. His apartment was just two blocks away.

"Stop here," he said suddenly. "In front of that house." He pointed at a ranch-style house with a For Sale sign in the front yard.

"What are we doing here?"

He opened the car door. "I want you to see this house."

"Why?" I killed the engine.

Axel bit down on a smile. "Please, just come inside. I have ideas."

We got out of the car. I followed as he walked up to the front steps and opened the door.

The house was vacant. "Ax, please tell me why we're breaking and entering."

"We aren't." He turned around and gave me a slightly nervous grin. "I talked to the real estate agent and she left it open for us. I want to buy this house, baby. We can all fit. There's three bedrooms upstairs, and in the basement there's a fourth one. It's kind of perfect for a moody teenager."

"Well, hell." I looked at the barren walls of the empty house. The place was big and seemed clean enough. But it hadn't seen a paint brush since the seventies. "I can't afford a house. I love that you think we can."

Axel rubbed his hands together. "I'm going to buy it."

"How? The down payment would be fifty grand. Your piggybank can't possibly have that kind of coin in it."

My boyfriend smiled at me. "True, but I'm getting some help from my mom. She wants to invest."

"What?" I looked more closely at him now, at the twinkle in his eye. "You're serious, aren't you?"

"Of course! Why else do you think I'd drag you into a vacant house? I want to make an offer, but first I need to know if you hate this place. There are other houses. Not many, but..."

I held up a hand. "How would this work?"

"My mother and I would buy the house, and we'd all move in. Not my mom," he amended quickly. "She's downsizing in Ohio to a condo. That's why she'll have cash to invest here. Her only requirement is that we buy a comfortable sofa bed for the times she visits."

I tried to picture that, but my head was busy exploding at all these new ideas. "But how would I pay you rent?"

Axel shrugged. "When the lawyers work out the child support, we'll talk then. Meanwhile, we can improve this house, Cax. It needs a lot of work—but not structurally. It's all painting and ripping out old wallpaper. New floors, maybe. I'm looking forward to it."

I took a deep breath against the tightness in my chest. "I don't know. There's so much up in the air for me. PhD programs take a *long* time, Ax..."

He came closer and hugged me. "But we have a long time," he whispered. "Stop panicking, baby. You need a place to live. The bank is going to be circling you like a shark soon. You said so yourself."

"He still hasn't paid this month's mortgage," I said, putting my chin on his shoulder. "I think he's trying to smoke us out. Can you believe that? His own kids."

He kissed my jaw. "Fuck 'im. The court will make him pay. And maybe it takes a year. But we'll be here, learning how to sand floorboards. Caleb and Josh are going to help us. Amy will help, too. My mom will come to stay for a little while. You're not alone. *We're* not alone."

"Can we really do this?" I whispered.

"Of course." He kissed me again. "What's the worst thing that could happen?"

"Bankruptcy? Duh."

Axel chuckling against my sensitive skin was the best feeling ever. "Can I show you the rest of the house now? Because you'll have to pick up Scotty in an hour."

"Yeah." I took a deep breath and stepped back. "Show me."

THE NEXT DAY I couldn't stop thinking about the house. Even as I stood in our old kitchen stirring pasta sauce at the stove, I took yet another mental tour of the other place.

In its current condition, the vacant house wasn't beautiful. But it had *so* much potential. The backyard was especially large, with space for a patio. *"And look! There's already a basketball hoop over the garage,"* Axel had pointed out.

For some reason, that detail made it seem real, because it made me picture a future there. Axel could teach Scotty how to dribble crossovers while I grilled the burgers. Mark could finish his homework at the kitchen counter (currently made of laminate, but we could eventually upgrade.)

I wanted that future so damn bad.

"The bank called again today looking for Dad," Jared said behind me. "But I think there's progress, because when I told the loan officer that Dad was in prison, he said, 'Oh, I see a note about that in the file.'"

I snorted. "That's progress? I guess you're right. At least it's made it into some corner of the file."

Jared stole a carrot stick from the heap I'd made on the serving platter. "What'll happen to this house if we don't pay the mortgage?"

"Either Dad will sell it, or the bank will take it," I said. "But we'll be okay. We'll go live somewhere else."

"Can't we just pay the mortgage?" Mark asked. I hadn't heard him come into the room. So far, Jared was the only one I'd spoken to about our current housing difficulties. He was old enough to figure out the problem himself.

"Well." I cleared my throat. "I can't pay the mortgage alone. I don't make enough money. And the court will probably make Dad pay it. But they won't get around to that for a while. Until after his trial."

"What are we going to do?" Mark asked, sounding about five years younger than he was. Sounding like a frightened child.

I turned to look him in the eye. "There are a few possibilities. I'm going to choose the best one."

"Like what?" He wasn't going to let it go.

"Grandma and Grandpa in Canada might end up helping us." Our mom's parents were deceased, but my father's were about a hundred years old and living in a nursing home. I hadn't spoken to them yet about what was going on, and I didn't know if my father had. But if we became truly destitute, I was going to petition them for help.

"I don't want to move to Canada," Mark said quickly, his brow furrowing.

"We're not," I said gently. "Moving is a last-place option. But it's possible I'll need to find a full-time job, and the Henning job market isn't all that big."

Mark cringed.

"There's one other idea." I turned off the pasta sauce to buy myself a moment. Mark and I had been circling each other these past two weeks. I'd made myself available to him, hoping he'd ask me questions about Axel or Amy or both. But he hadn't. Meanwhile, we'd seen Axel twice—once for a pizza dinner and once when Axel came over for lunch on the weekend. Both times, Mark had ignored him.

But now I was going for it. I was going to bring it up, and he was going to have to deal. "Axel wants to buy a house. We might all live there."

Mark dropped his eyes. "Where?" he asked.

"Newbury Street."

He rubbed a rough corner of the tiled floor with his toe. "Is that the best option?" he asked.

"Probably," I said quietly. "Unless Dad does something generous and signs over this house to us. And even then we couldn't afford it."

Mark chewed his lip. "But we can afford it if we live with Axel?"

"Yeah," I said quietly. "We'd pay him back when we could. But he's not going to kick us to the curb. And you could stay in school with your friends."

"Can we eat now?" Jared asked. "I'm starved, and I have homework."

The moment broken, I turned back to the stove and relit the fire under the sauce.

"Pasta again?" Mark complained. It's not like my father had made the boys terrific meals. But he used to buy lots of frozen crap that I couldn't afford. They were used to nuking whichever pizza or burrito struck their fancy.

I tore the top off a box of pasta and poured it into the boiling water. "There's something you should know about Axel," I said. "He's a fabulous cook." I wondered what he'd think of me talking up his cooking to win over Mark. I pictured him in his apartment kitchen, checking the chicken in the oven. He'd probably be okay with it, actually. After all, it was *his* idea to live with the entire Williams brood.

"Really?"

"Yeah," I said. "He's a real pro."

Mark stole a carrot stick. "Maybe he can teach you. If we all live in one house."

Warmth bloomed in my chest at the sound of those words, and the fact that he'd said them so easily. I wanted to grin and grab him in a hug, but that wouldn't fly with a teenager. "Maybe he can," I said instead. "Maybe you can learn, too."

"Probably not," Mark grumbled. Then he wandered toward the family room.

I felt my shoulders relax by a fraction of a degree. Because this might just really work.

CHAPTER TWENTY-SIX

Axel

The day after I showed the house to Cax, I finally went back to work at the athletic department.

I was still two weeks away from getting the cast off my arm, but otherwise I was doing much better. My ribs felt mostly normal, except when I coughed or sneezed. And more importantly, the vision in my right eye was back to normal.

"Get yer ass back in the chair!" Boz yelled when I walked into the office. "I'm killing myself trying to cover hockey and basketball."

"Nice to see you, too, Boz."

He smirked at me. "I'm, like, responsible for you now, right?"

"What?" I set the cup of coffee I'd bought down on the desk. "What do you mean?"

"You know—because I saved your life."

"How do you figure?"

"Carrying that stretcher, man. Do I own you now, like a slave? Are you going to name your children after me?" He spun his desk chair.

And to think I'd missed this place. "Truth is, I can't get my boyfriend pregnant. But Boz sounds like a good name for a dog."

He grasped his chest in mock horror. "A *dog?*"

"That's really the best you can hope for from Cax and I."

"I should have left you bleeding in the woods."

"Then you'd have to cover hockey and basketball by yourself. You might accidentally work more than forty hours a week."

He picked up a Barmuth Bears sweat band off his desk and threw it at me. "Good point, asshole."

"I might be persuaded to take you out for lunch, later, though." I threw the sweat band back, bouncing it off his forehead.

Boz tucked his hands behind his head and grinned. "That'll do. Now help me plan a family night at the hockey stadium. Can I just copy your press release?"

"Sure, pal. As long as you remember to put the word 'hockey' wherever I wrote 'basketball.'"

"You could do that part for me."

"You're going to milk this whole 'lifesaving' thing, aren't you?" I gave the word air quotes.

"Uh-huh."

I turned on my dusty computer and started searching for the press release.

THE DAY WENT BY QUICKLY. It felt good to think about work again, as opposed to all the big questions in my life.

I missed Cax, though. And I wasn't sure it was a good sign that I hadn't heard from him after our big discussion in the vacant house on Newbury Street.

At home that evening, I sent him a text. *Can we talk?*

212

He came back with: *Can I call you around ten? Pajamas optional.*

Of course.

I was awfully tired, and staying up until ten proved harder than it should have. I ate a piece of lasagna and watched some sports highlights on television. Then I got into bed to wait for Cax's call.

Unfortunately, ten o'clock came and went without my phone ringing. At ten minutes past, I texted him again. *Are you free now?*

There was no response. But a minute later, someone knocked on my door.

And, goddamn it, I actually experienced a shiver of fear. There was no reason to feel unsafe in my apartment. The only man in town who'd ever wanted to hurt me was locked up. But the subconscious is a bitch sometimes. "Who is it?" I called.

"Just some guy," Cax's voice said from behind the door. "Some guy who wants to get you naked."

I shivered again for an entirely different reason. Then I hustled over to the door and opened it as quickly as humanly possible. "Hi," I breathed as Cax came in, bringing the January chill with him.

He kissed me once, quickly. "Get back in bed, babe. It's cold. And that's where I want you, anyway."

Heat flared in my groin as I obeyed him, crossing the room and climbing into my bed again. We'd always lacked for time alone, and this was the best kind of gift. "You left Jared in charge?"

"All three of them are asleep. I left a note on the kitchen table saying where I'd gone. But my plan is to go home around seven tomorrow morning, so I can get Scotty up for school." He stood over me beside the bed, shifting his weight from foot to foot. "Is that okay?"

"That is better than okay. Now get over here."

He grinned, those hazel eyes smiling at me. He shucked off his coat and put his hands to the buttons of his oxford shirt.

"Let me do that," I said, my voice husky. "Take off your jeans, though."

His long fingers manipulated his belt, and I felt myself growing hard. I'd always wanted this man, and here he was, taking off his clothes for me. I yanked my T-shirt over my head, but it got stuck on my fucking cast.

"Let me," he said, kneeling on my bed, easing it off. "Oh, yeah," he said with a sigh, straddling my thighs. He tossed the T-shirt away and leaned down to kiss my chest.

I tipped my head back against the pillows and sighed with happiness. He tongued my nipple and I groaned. "Best idea you ever had, Caxy."

"One of 'em," he agreed, kissing his way up to my neck. "I want you to fuck me. I've been thinking about it all day."

The words drew a moan from my lips. "Damn, I like hearing you say it almost as much as I like doing it."

He lay down beside me, taking care to avoid my broken arm. He put his lips beside my ear. "Spent my whole life being careful what I said," he whispered. "But now I just want to shout it from the rooftops."

"Go for it," I breathed. My body was humming with arousal as Cax let his fingers drift across my belly. "Tell me more of what you want."

"Mmm," he said, and my dick twitched at the breathy sound. "You're going to lay on your back, and I'm going to ride you while you fuck me."

"Jesus," I whispered as an electric current of lust ran straight from my ear to my balls. "What else?"

"You're going to come in my ass, and I'm going to come all over your chest while I suck on your tongue."

214

"*Ungh*," I gasped. "Get the lube. Quick."

He chuckled and dove toward the bedside table. How was this my life? Cax, the man of my dreams, had somehow become acquainted with his inner dirty-talker. I lubed up my fingers as he turned toward the foot of the bed and presented his ass to me. "I don't know what's got into you," I said, stroking my fingers into his crease. "But I like it." I penetrated him gently with my forefinger, and he gave a happy gasp.

"Just needed you," he panted as I began to prep him. "I don't want to be quiet anymore. Because...ahh." He dropped his head to the bedspread. "Fuck first, talk later," he mumbled.

"Deal," I ground out. Fingering him was making me hard as a board. The number of times we'd been naked together was still quite small, but it didn't feel that way. At that moment, I could swear we'd been lovers for years. The trust we had for each other was like a cocoon surrounding the bed. I sat up straighter and leaned forward so that I could kiss the muscles on his beautiful back.

"Yeah," he breathed. "Want you so bad."

Holy...all the amazing dirty talk was going to be hell on my self-control. I concentrated on the matter at hand, stretching him until he was pressing back on my fingers. Until he was ready for me.

"Spin around, baby," I said, fixing the pillows behind myself, sitting up a little bit.

He turned his body around and rose up on his knees on either side of me. The view up his gorgeous chest was breath-taking. And his perfect, hard cock was *almost* close enough to taste. I looked away to hunt for the condom and to calm down for a second, too.

"Ax, you know you're disease-free, right?"

The question halted me in my tracks. "Yeah. I've been tested. Why?" I looked up into his hazel eyes.

He smiled down at me. "I don't see how we need that condom. You're safe and I'm a monk."

"Wow." I let out a whole lot of air. "Except I'm going to last about thirty seconds if we go bareback."

Cax grinned. "Sounds like fun." He reached for the lube, opened the top, then drizzled some right onto my dick. He slicked me up while I practically passed out from anticipation.

I closed my eyes, just trying to survive it. "Not kidding, babe. This won't be my most impressive moment. You're fucking killing me right now."

His grin turned evil. He walked his knees forward until he was in position.

Then? He lined me up and sank down slowly onto my dick.

The most beautiful tight heat enveloped me, and I found myself panting through the incredible sensation. "Oh...sweet Jesus," I huffed. "So tight."

He dropped his elbows onto the bed, and covered my mouth with his. We kissed hungrily. Desperately. As if this were the last kiss we'd ever have.

It wouldn't be. And that made it even sweeter.

"Oh fuck," I moaned into his mouth. "Fuck yourself on me, baby. I want it."

He gave his hips a little push—just enough to remind me how good it was going to be.

"Oh please oh please oh please," I chanted between kisses. "Want to fuck you. Need to come."

He straightened up a little bit, smiling down at me. "Not just yet, babe. But soon."

With a giant groan, I tried rolling my hips. That gave me something, but it wasn't quite enough.

Finally, Cax took mercy on me. With his hands on the bed, he began to fuck himself on me in short, slow strokes. After a few of these, he gave a giant groan. "Oh, Axel. I love you inside me."

"I love you everywhere," I sighed, giving myself over to it. I slipped a hand onto his cock and stroked once, and he gasped.

"That's...ahh." He sighed, picking up his pace. "This is...I can put you right where I need you." His eyes squeezed shut with pleasure. "It's perfect."

It was. I stroked him again, my thumb brushing his cock-head, trailing through the slickness where he was leaking for me. I relaxed for a minute, breathing deeply while he rode me. But I wanted it too badly to wait much longer. There was nothing between us—no condom, no troubles. This was mine to enjoy, and I couldn't hold out anymore. "Come for me, hon. Kiss me and come for me."

On a moan, he dropped his eager mouth onto mine. I pushed my tongue inside, and he sucked on it. Once. Twice. I felt all our troubles drop away on his lusty sigh. I squeezed his cock, and that's when I felt it starting. He shuddered on a thrust. Then his ass clamped down on my throbbing cock, and he began to erupt in my hand and moan into my mouth all at once.

With a growl, I wrenched my hips up. My balls hitched and tightened and then it was all over but the crying. My climax roared through my veins as I unloaded all my tensions into his hard, willing body.

A few moments later we lay side by side, and I tried to pull him closer.

"Your ribs," he mumbled.

"They're fine. Get over here."

Clumsily, he heaved himself partly onto my sticky body. "We need to take that bedroom over the garage," he panted. "So the boys can't hear us when we fuck."

"You mean..." I lit up inside with excitement. "In the house down the street?"

He nodded against my face. Then he kissed my cheek.

"I can't wait to live there with you," I said.

"Me too. Doesn't mean I'm not still worried about the money."

I gave him a little pinch. "It's only money. I know we don't have quite enough of it. But I don't have enough of you in my life, either. And that's the bigger problem."

"Agreed," he said quietly. "I kind of hinted tonight that you might be part of our future. Mark took it better than I thought."

Stroking his hair, I pulled him a little closer. "I don't know Mark very well. But your brothers love you so much. And if they're living in a house where nobody's yelling, they're going to notice that life is pretty good."

"Hope so," he said. "I'm going for it either way, though. Even if Mark has trouble with it. I just don't want him acting like a dick to you. That's what worries me."

I thought about that for a minute. "He might. But I've been an out gay man for years, and I don't think there's anything he could say to me that I haven't already heard. And he's got *scared kid* written all over him, babe. I can handle him until he forgets to be scared."

Cax smiled against my face. "One more thing? I may have mentioned that you're a fabulous cook. And he liked the sound of that."

This caused me to hoot with laughter. "You're pimping out my chicken with garlic, feta and lemon?"

"Yes." Now we were both laughing. "Sorry. I'm just really desperate to have this work."

"Uh-huh. I see how it really is." I pinched his ass. "Kidding aside, I'll cook a feast for that kid if it will win him over."

"It might. It's true what they say. The path to a man's heart..."

"Is with blowjobs."

Cax snorted. "The path to a *boy's* heart is through his stomach. If I'm living in your house, you have to let me buy all the groceries. Those boys can *eat*."

"Our house," I said softly.

"Our house," he repeated. "In the meantime, can I use your rented shower?"

"Go for it."

Cax got up and disappeared for a couple of minutes. He came back wearing my towel and carrying a washcloth. Sitting beside me on the bed, he lowered the warm cloth to my chest. And when I tried to take over, he pushed my hand out of the way. "Let me. Any day now you'll be all healed up, and you won't need my help anymore."

"I'll always want your help," I said, running a hand down his strong arm.

He leaned over to kiss me once on the belly. "Good. How was your first day back, anyway? I was too busy sexing you up to ask."

I closed my eyes as the washcloth made another pass. "Don't remember now. Too tired. Too sexed up."

Cax chuckled and kissed my clean skin once again. "Sleep. I'm going to borrow your toothbrush and come to bed."

"'Kay. Love you."

"Love you."

He clicked off the bedside lamp, and I dozed until a warm, comfortable body pressed in beside me.

Then I slept, knowing everything was finally going well.

Caxton

Nine Months Later

"The doorbell is ringing," Mark said. My brother lay flat on his back on the floor, a paperback thriller held over his head.

"Then get it, you lazy oaf," I prompted. "I'm up to my ears in potato peels, here."

"I'll do it," Axel's mother said, wiping her hands on her apron.

"You shouldn't have to, Ann," I protested, but she was already on her way to the door. I took two steps away from the kitchen island so that I could give Mark a little kick at his ankle. "Nice manners, kid. Way to go."

His only response was to turn the page.

I went back to the task at hand—prepping potatoes. This past year Axel had worked hard to teach me to cook. And I'd worked hard learning. Cooking was fun when it involved following my hot boyfriend around the kitchen.

And while I wished Mark would have slightly better manners, I wasn't going to make a big deal about it. Because his comfort level with our new family situation had drastically improved since the early days. He regularly invited his friends over now. And last week I'd heard him introduce Axel to his wrestling teammate as "Cax's boyfriend."

It had been tempting to say, "See, did that kill you?" But I didn't do that, and I'm sure he was grateful.

"Hey guys! Happy Thanksgiving!"

I turned to see Jason enter the kitchen, carrying three bottles of wine. "Hey, man. Thanks for bringing those."

"It's the least I could do." He set them down on the island and looked around. "I love what you've done back here. This is looking great."

"Thanks. Caleb did a lot of it." Our friend and neighbor had helped us tear down the wall between the kitchen and the den, so the floor plan could be more of a family space, like the old house.

"Will we see them today?" Jason asked, shrugging off his coat.

"Not until later," I said. "He and Josh are having dinner with their family in Cheshire. But they might stop by for a drink this evening."

"Where's Axel?"

"In here!" Axel yelled from the dining room. "I'm trying to figure out if the fireplace flu works, or if I'm just going to smoke us out."

"Need a hand?" Jason offered.

"Nah—I think I got it." He appeared a minute later, smiling, smelling a little like smoke. "Happy Thanksgiving, man." He shook Jason's hand. "Glad you could join us."

Axel's mother joined us in the kitchen again. "Boys, we need to get those potatoes boiling. This turkey is almost done. And Axel has to put his famous pretzel rolls into the oven."

Suddenly, Mark sat up. "Axel made pretzel rolls?"

My eyes drifted over to Axel, who winked. "He sure did."

"Awesome," my middle brother said, putting a hand to his stomach.

"You get one only if you set the table," Axel's mother said. "And Cax—we need those potatoes."

"Sorry." I went back to the task at hand. "I'm a good worker, but I'm not fast."

Axel held out his hand. "Can I take over? There's only one peeler and..." He grinned.

"I'm not offended." I handed it over. "I'll quarter them."

In the time it took me to say those three words, Axel had seized a potato and peeled half of it. "Deal."

THIRTY MINUTES LATER, Ann had managed to get the boys to set the table. Jason and I were pouring drinks. Ann and Axel moved around the kitchen like a pair of skilled dancers, always anticipating each other's moves.

"Wow," Jason said, watching Axel cook. "I knew he was a catch."

That made me blush. I'd never say so out loud, but I didn't like knowing that Jason had once asked Axel out.

"When are we going to catch someone for you?" Axel asked as he whisked gravy. My eyes were glued to the muscles flexing in his forearm as he did this. There was nothing sexier than a hunk of a man making dinner. Nothing.

"I don't know..." Jason raised a hand to the back of his neck, and I thought I saw his cheeks heat.

"Really?" Axel cackled. "Who is he?"

"I'll tell you later," he muttered. "What else can I do?"

"Wrangle the boys to the table," Ann said. "I'm done carving."

"I'll do that," I said. "BOYS! FOOD!"

There was an instant pounding of feet toward the table in the other room.

She laughed. "I'd forgotten how hungry boys are when they're growing." She lifted the platter of turkey, which looked amazing. "Okay, let's eat."

We all sat down, and miraculously my brothers waited for Ann to say a thirty-second prayer before they lunged for the food.

I scanned the contented faces at the table and got a lump in my throat. A year ago this scene would have been impossible for me—a friendly meal with family, my boyfriend at the table.

"Cax?" Axel touched my arm. "Aren't you eating?"

"Um, yep," I said, taking the bowl of stuffing he handed me. "Just got a little distracted there for a second."

His mother shot me a warm look from across the table. "I have an important question. What does the Williams clan do about dessert? Do you eat it right away, or should there be a lull in between?"

"Oh, there's a lull," Jared said, passing the mashed potatoes. "But this year we can skip the part where Dad makes Scotty cry because he can't throw a spiral."

"I can too throw a spiral," Scotty argued.

Jared smirked, but Scotty failed to notice, luckily.

"Do they, um..." Scotty's eyes darted to mine. "Is there Thanksgiving in prison?"

"Yeah," I said softly. Truly, I had no idea. But probably, right? "He's okay, Scott. He'd rather be here with you than in there. But that's just the way it is."

"Shouldn't have beat up Axel, then," Jared said before shoving a giant bite of turkey into his mouth.

Axel raised his eyes to mine, as if wondering whether I'd pursue that line of discussion. But I just shook my head. "Which football teams are we rooting for today?"

"Patriots. Duh," Mark said to his plate.

"Duh," Jason echoed, and everybody laughed. Even Mark.

HOURS later we were sitting around the table again. It had been cleared of food and then dessert. Jared and Mark were out at the movies with friends, and Scotty was either asleep or playing with his iPod in his sleeping bag on the floor of Jared's room. He'd given up his bed for Ann while she stayed with us.

Axel's mom had turned in already.

That left Axel and me, Jason, and Caleb and Josh. We sat there with fresh glasses of wine trying not to groan from eating too much food.

"Maggie sent us home with a pile of leftovers," Josh said, swirling the liquid in his glass. "It's the best of both worlds. We don't have to cook Thanksgiving dinner, and we still have turkey sandwiches for three days."

"You really have cracked the code," Jason said, lifting his glass to Josh. "I salute you."

"Do we get to hear about your mystery boyfriend now?" Axel asked. "I've waited, like, hours."

Jason propped his head in one hand. "There's no mystery boyfriend. But I do have a really hot neighbor. He lives next door to the new house." Jason had just moved—finally—to Merryline to be closer to his office and clientele.

"How much do we know about the hot neighbor?" Axel inquired.

"Well..." Jason laughed. "There was an incident."

"A naked incident?" Caleb asked.

"Yeah." Jason sighed. "Much fun was had. But when I picked him up at The Shaft I sort of left out the fact that I lived next door. And afterward he was kind of pissed off about that."

"Why?" Josh asked.

"Not sure." Jason frowned. "I guess it could seem sort of stalkerish. But we were both on the same page. It was just a hookup. A really awesome hookup."

"What does he look like?" Caleb asked. "What's your type?"

"Not sure I have a type. But he's a rough-looking bearded guy. Think lumbersexual. He'd fit in better in the woods than he does in my neighborhood."

"Are we going to see this house?" I asked.

"Anytime. I have guest rooms. But only one of them has a bed in it."

"We could go to The Shaft," Axel said, moving his leg under the table beside mine.

"That is a terrible name for a bar," Josh said.

"The worst," I agreed, stroking Axel's foot with mine.

"Well." Jason pushed back his chair. "I have to head home. And it isn't because you're grilling me. But it's late, and I have a long drive."

"You could crash at our place," Caleb offered.

"I'm gonna drive home," Jason insisted. "I'm listening to a sexy audio book and I turned it off at a good part. Makes the miles fly by. And it's the only play I'm getting tonight. Unlike you people."

"I think I'm too full for sex," Caleb grunted, standing up, too. "Let's go home, babe. I need to hibernate like a bear."

We saw our friends out, then took the last of the glasses to the kitchen. A few minutes later we climbed into our new, king-sized bed and met in the middle. "I can't get it on with my mom in the house," Axel whispered.

I burst out laughing. "Okay." After we'd moved in together, it had taken me a little while to get used to having sex under the same roof as my brothers. I did it anyway, but at the beginning it seemed risky.

But not anymore. These days we got plenty. Which is why Axel didn't mind that a little making out was all that would happen tonight.

"Not too tight," he groaned as I hugged him. "I'm so full. I might explode."

"That's so sexy." Chuckling, I kissed him.

He wrapped his arms around me and sighed. "Explosions aside, that was an awesome holiday."

"It was," I agreed. "But now starts the march toward Christmas. I don't know what to get you."

"Nothing," he said quickly. "I already have everything I want."

The same was true for me, but instead of saying so, I teased him. "Well, I guess I'll have to return that blowjob I was going to give you."

He pinched my ass. "You'll give it to me anyway."

"True."

"Happy Thanksgiving, Cax."

"Back at you, babe."

We shared another kiss, and then went to sleep in each other's arms.

The End

∾

Thank you! If you enjoyed *Hello Forever*, click here to find more MM romance by Sarina Bowen. Or turn the page for a list of titles.

Be sure to sign up for Sarina's mailing list so you won't miss a thing!

ALSO BY SARINA BOWEN

LOOKING FOR MORE LGBTQ ROMANCE?

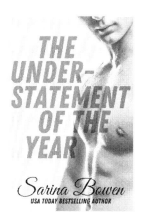

Goodbye Paradise

Roommate

The Understatement of the Year

Him by Sarina Bowen & Elle Kennedy

Us by Sarina Bowen & Elle Kennedy

Top Secret by Sarina Bowen & Elle Kennedy

Also: TRUE NORTH

Bittersweet

Steadfast

Keepsake

Bountiful

Speakeasy

Made in the USA
Monee, IL
27 November 2023

47555494R00131